ROCK
PAPER
KILLERS

ROCK PAPER KILLERS

ALEXIA MASON

SIMON & SCHUSTER

First published in Great Britain in 2022 by Simon & Schuster UK Ltd

3 5 7 9 10 8 6 4 2

Simon & Schuster UK Ltd
1st Floor, 222 Gray's Inn Road
London
WC1X 8HB

www.simonandschuster.co.uk
www.simonandschuster.com.au
www.simonandschuster.co.in

Simon & Schuster Australia, Sydney
Simon & Schuster India, New Delhi

A CIP catalogue record for this book is available from the British Library.

PB ISBN 978-1-3985-0878-1
eBook ISBN 978-1-3985-0879-8
eAudio ISBN 978-1-3985-0880-4

Printed and bound by CPI Group (UK) Ltd, Croydon, CR0 4YY

MIX
Paper from
responsible sources
FSC® C171272

To the incomparable Rachel Denwood

Every summer, thousands of Irish teenagers go to the Gaeltacht – the regions where Irish is still spoken as the first language, and where colleges offer intensive courses to secondary school students in preparation for their final exams. While most Irish people learn Irish at school, few speak it or use it on a regular basis.

Rinne mé é
Rinne tú é
Rinne sé/sí é
Rinne sibh é
Rinneamar é
Rinne siad é

I did it
You did it
He/She did it
You (pl.) did it
We did it
They did it

PROLOGUE

We stood
at the top of the
rock watching her fall
then we walked back down
with the truth we would tell if
anyone asked us what happened
up there because friends are in safe
hands with friends and we really were
we lied so it was an accident and that night
even though we reached the base of the rock
the truth was our descent had started weeks ago

PART ONE - ROCK

1

Amber stood in the darkened kitchen waiting for the water in the clear glass kettle to boil, absently clutching the handle of the cafetière. She became aware of the tightness of her grip, released it, and let out a long, relieved breath. It was six a.m. and she was free. Any time her mother was sleeping, she was free. The rolling forecast of doom was switched off.

Amber's gaze moved to the calendar on the side of the fridge, freshly turned to August, the first three weeks boxed off in red marker with *Gaeltacht!* written across it. It wasn't there a week ago. It was a sudden reaction to an email sent by the school telling parents that Mr McQuaid, the Irish teacher, wouldn't be coming back in September. In Amber's case – her final year. The year she would sit the Leaving Cert, which decided what university she would go to. Within days, she and four of her friends were late-

3

breaking additions to an intensive Irish language course in Galway that the ninety other students had probably been signed up to for years. The only difference was those other ninety would be staying with Irish-speaking host families nearby, and Amber and her friends – Rupert, Kelly, Lockie and LB – would be staying on campus, in 'luxury accommodation' according to LB's dad who made it all happen. (He was a musician, a rock star, he knew the owner – and he was going to do everything he could to give his daughter her best chance.)

Amber reached up to open the cupboard door, and an image flashed through her mind of the kettle coming to a violent boil under her arm, melting her skin.

'Stop.'

She said it out loud. Sometimes, she had to. Like she was talking to someone else, which she kind of was. Amber loved her mother, but not her mother's fears. They were like ticks she flicked off herself and onto Amber. They burrowed into her brain. Amber pulled open the drawer and the blade of a kitchen knife shone.

'Stop. Oh my God.' Amber grabbed a spoon and closed the drawer. She walked back to the kettle and stared at the water bubbling wildly as it boiled. She loved water, loved its flowing freedom. She dreamed about soaring over waterfalls, breaking the churning surface, plunging into a quiet, contained darkness that felt like home. Or deep under the sea, moving like an eel, coiling and uncoiling around everything she thought was beautiful, through the broken portholes and cleaved metal of shipwrecks. Even shipwrecks can be beautiful. Rupert got it. Rupert let things breathe and be. Amber's mother needed things to make sense through her eyes and would never think to adjust her vision. Instead, she tried to adjust all the parts of Amber she didn't understand, as if one day everything would click into place.

Amber carried her mug up to the bedroom and went to the shelf where she kept her tarot and oracle card decks. She put the mug down, chose two oracle card decks, paused, then added a third. She scanned her shelf of crystals, picking whichever ones called to her and slipping them into a purple velvet drawstring bag. She turned to her desk where a selenite sphere, white and opaque, was mounted on a wooden stand. It was a heavy and cold handful that always warmed her heart – it was like holding the moon. She picked it up, wrapped it carefully in a sweatshirt, and tucked it into the middle of her rucksack. She was about to tie it closed when she remembered who else would be coming to Irish college. She picked up an ebony bracelet – silver clasp, shining beads of black obsidian.

For protection against negative energies.

Rupert Gore-Graves ducked in front of the mirror at the top of the stairs and, using gel and a wide-toothed comb, worked his thick, glossy, rich-red hair into a thoughtful arrangement of definable ridges in keeping with his look.

'Who are we today?' he knew Amber would ask when they met later.

'American Psycho,' he would answer, and she would see that – the slicked-back hair, the clean shave, the clenched jaw, the perfect white teeth and shirt, red braces, and, well, shorts because it was summer. Preppie, tailored and navy. And brown loafers. Then they would kiss on each cheek – proper kisses, lips on skin, not like Kelly's kisses that were literally air. But like the air of a silent secret she was breathing into you as her mouth swept past your ear.

Rupert went into his bedroom and looked with pride at his suitcase, open on the bed: clothing and footwear impeccably arranged. English language books – poetry and ghosts – in Irish language covers, wedged so neatly around them that only a savage would examine and confiscate them.

Rupert's father was waiting for him at the gate at the end of the very long laneway that led from their manor house to the road, his grey hair neatly combed, the sleeves of his flannel shirt rolled up to the elbows, the white hair on his arms lifting in the warm breeze.

'It will be unimaginable without you,' he said as Rupert approached.

'Everything is imaginable,' said Rupert. He gave his father a broad smile. His father's matched it.

'I love those sweeping, buoyant thoughts of yours, Rupe. The house will be terribly empty without them.'

'You know it's forbidden to lay any psychological burdens on your child,' said Rupert. 'Particularly when you're the banisher.'

'Good Lord – the banisher! Does that make you the banshee?'

'That's appalling,' said Rupert.

'If I spoke the language, I'd keep you here and teach you myself. You know that.'

'It's only three weeks,' said Rupert. 'And I do know that.' His brown eyes shone with love.

'It's not the nicest of languages, Irish, is it?' said his father. 'Quite harsh. Lots of "icks" and "ocks" and "chucks" and "coos" and . . . farmyard sounds, really.'

'Don't let the neighbours hear you,' said Rupert. 'As an English gentleman farmer landowner—'

'Charmer of local beauty,' said his father. He flipped open his battered leather wallet and Rupert saw the faded image of his mother, captured a year before she died. She was only twenty-six. 'Scandalous decades younger than me,' his father used to joke.

He rubbed his thumb across the photo.

'The Irish girl who stole my heart,' he said. 'And gave it back to me, bigger.' He nodded at Rupert.

'Oh my God, Dad – adorable.'

His father handed him two fifty-euro notes. Rupert handed one back. 'Don't be ridiculous.' He blew a kiss at his mother's photo. 'I never knew your fluency, nor will I. But I will toil in its honour.' He looked at his dad. 'And yours too, I hope you know.'

His father smiled. 'My kind boy, always concerned about feelings he wouldn't dream of hurting.' He nodded. 'Right, well – your chariot awaits.'

A horn beeped, and Rupert looked to where their elderly neighbour, Páidí, was getting out of his battered red, mud-splattered car, beaming at them both, reaching out a hand for Rupert's suitcase.

'Not at all,' said Rupert, about to walk around to the boot.

'Let him,' said his father, quietly. Rupert did. His father was always gentle in his redirects. He had told him that there was dignity for Páidí in earning the 'few bob' he paid him for the errands and odd jobs he did on the estate.

'Right,' said his father. 'Time to . . .'

They both nodded.

'You'll be able to speak to Páidí in his native tongue by the time you get back.'

'Manage your expectations,' said Rupert, as he settled into the front seat and arranged his long legs in the passenger footwell, using his loafers to gently work a hole in a layer of miscellaneous plastic soft drinks bottles.

He took one last look out of the window at his father.

Englishman Leaning On Farm Gate. Summer. Kildare.

Rupert liked to caption scenes as if they were paintings. Mostly in his head. Sometimes out loud. He waved goodbye to his father, who was wiping away a tear. Rupert's heart surged. He wanted to jump back out and give him another hug, but Páidí was reversing like the maniac he was, and sentiment would never slow him. Rupert braced himself for half an hour of listening to Páidí talk GAA on the drive to the train station.

To Rupert, the Gaelic Athletic Association was great, hurling was great, Gaelic football was great. Great unknowns.

'I'm more a G-A-Y fan, myself,' Rupert wanted to say. Except he wasn't sure that that was the truth, either. That he was *a fan*. There was feeling gay, and then there were the feelings about the feelings. You're meant to love and accept who you are these days. But Rupert loved how his father loved him more. What if it stopped? He had never heard his father say anything homophobic. Not once. But, still . . . what if it stopped?

Lotus 'LB' Behan ran her hand down the side of her black stallion, Guinness. Tears welled in her eyes.

'Ooh,' said LB. 'Bit emosh, Guinn.'

She tipped her head back and sent the tears down the sides of her rosy cheeks.

Her father came up behind her.

'Lotus Behan,' he said, putting an arm around her shoulder. LB patted his hand, turned around, and smiled. 'Hey,' she said gently. 'You look tired.'

'Me? I always look tired.' He smiled, but it didn't quite reach his eyes. 'Gonna miss you, LB,' he said.

'Gonna miss you too,' said LB.

LB was used to missing him, but this was different – she was the one leaving him behind. At home. In Dublin. And even though she hadn't expected him to be there – the family were meant to be on their annual vacation in the south of France – she felt like she was missing out on having him around the house. When he could cook her awful breakfasts but entertain her away from really noticing. But she didn't say anything because she didn't want to guilt him, and she didn't want to seem ungrateful.

'Thank you for arranging all this,' said LB.

Her dad laughed. 'I did something right with you,' he said. 'The idea of me thanking the old man for a trip to the Gaeltacht . . .' He patted LB's head. 'Mind you, if it had been a five-star experience . . .'

LB laughed.

'Though the place is only half done,' said her dad. 'Does that make it a two-point-five?'

LB groaned. 'Whatever it's like, I promise you I'll nail the H1.'

'Are they giving you exams? In the summer?'

'Yes!' said LB. 'That's why it's so insane!'

'OK – do me one favour,' said her dad, 'and don't tell your mom I asked – she thinks I don't listen to her. H1 – is that the same as an A? How many points is that?'

'Dad!' said LB, faux-frustrated. 'Forget about As. H1 is ninety to a hundred per cent. And that gets you a hundred points. H2—'

Her dad gave her the 'wrap it up' signal. 'You're going to lose your old man. You know I subcontract all the numbers stuff to Ash. Mind you, she's got a bit of a blind spot when it comes to Kelly.'

LB laughed.

'Daughters,' said her dad, shaking his head. He winked. 'OK . . . go on . . .'

'OK – all you need to know,' said LB, 'is that I have to

get all H1s if I want to do veterinary science in UCD. It's six hundred points.'

'And – tell me again – what's wrong with being an off-the-rails celebrity offspring?' said her dad. 'OK – one more question. What's the H about?'

'Dad! Same as it was for you, Mom said. Higher! And there's O for Ordinary.'

'Now you're talking,' said her dad. He held a hand to his chest. 'To the Ordinary man—'

'Who conquered the world,' said LB.

Her dad smiled, pulled her into a hug, and kissed the top of her blonde head.

'Listen, why don't I give you a lift?' he said, stepping back.

'To Galway?'

'Yeah,' said her dad. 'Why not? Fire up the chopper, land you on the grounds in style.'

LB's eyes widened with horror.

Her dad laughed. 'Fine. I'll drive you there. Like the Ordinary man I am.'

Marcus 'Lockie' Loughnane, lightly tanned, frowny, full-mouthed, was stretched across the back seat of the Kildare to Galway bus, rubbing his belly under his rugby shirt, scrolling through his phone. It started to ring. *Private Number.* He hesitated, then answered. He sat up and listened, then sat up straighter again.

'Sorry – what?' said Lockie, leaning forward, chest out like a bull ready to charge. 'With all due respect, Mr—'

The caller was shouting over him so loud people were glancing back.

Lockie angled his body away, and spoke as quietly as he could. 'I don't know what you're talking about, but—'

He was shouted down again, and listened, open-mouthed, hand on his head, clutching a fistful of hair.

'With all due respect, Mr Hogan—'

The shouting went on, but Lockie talked over him. 'I did not send any photos.' He paused. 'It can't be my face.' He listened. 'I don't know!' He paused. 'No, I have a lot of respect. It's just I'm on a bus. I'm going to the Gaeltacht. So . . . so I won't be around anyway.'

The bus hit a bump hard, and as the phone jerked a little away from Lockie's ear, he hung up.

The phone rang again – this time *Dad* was flashing on it. Lockie rolled his eyes, picked up and listened.

'It was a private number!' said Lockie. 'How was I supposed to know?' He paused, listened again. Anger swept across his face. 'Well, I don't care what your solicitor buddy says!' His father was shouting over him. 'I know that!' hissed Lockie. 'I wouldn't want to see that either if I was him. But it wasn't me.' He listened again.

'"Stay out of trouble" – I'm not five . . . What? . . . Dad, I've no interest in other girls. I love Clare! And she loves me. Yeah: love! You know – that feeling *you* get when you open your wallet? And what your solicitor buddy feels when that fat fee drops into his account?'

His father was bellowing down the phone. Lockie stared up at the ceiling. 'No. THANK you, thank you. Thank you *so* much. I really, really, REALLY appreciate it. Money well spent. I LOVE IRISH.'

Kelly Warner sat on her bed beside her half-packed suitcase, holding a pile of clothes on her lap.

'For God's sake, Kelly,' said her mother, 'it's three weeks. Suck it up! What is so hard? You've been doing Irish since you were four years old! I told you – I'm not doing another year of this. Whingeing and moaning and "write me a note". Take some responsibility! And it's not like you're slumming it. I don't know if you realise how ungrateful you sound.'

She grabbed the pile of clothes from Kelly and pressed it hard into the suitcase. 'Why am I even doing this?'

'I don't know,' said Kelly. But she did know. It was because her mother never thought she could do anything right. Every time her mother walked into a room, Kelly felt watched, waiting in the dead-air pause before the judgement came, that flash on her mother's face that said, 'WRONG, KELLY! And you need to know it.' What was the point in doing anything if her mother was around to take over?

'You're a brat!' said her mom, coming out of the en suite holding matching bottles of shampoo and conditioner. 'Sorry, but you're in a thirty-grand-a-year private school, living in— Just *look* at this house that I kill myself for! But nothing is good enough.' She held up the bottles. 'Are you taking these?'

'No!' said Kelly. 'I've already packed my toiletries.' She pointed to a cherry-red carry-on bag by the door.

'Are you joking me?' said her mother. She sprung for it, and Kelly sprung after her.

'Mom – don't!' She tried to grab it, as her mother tried to swing it away.

'Leave it!' said Kelly. 'It's heavy.'

'Yeah, because you've emptied the bathroom into it!' said her mom, laying it down on the ground. She clicked it open, and looked up at Kelly. 'Would you get a grip? You're going to *school* – hate to break it to you. Where do you think you'll get the time to –' she plucked out a white LED face mask – 'reduce your fine lines and wrinkles?'

'Mom, stop!' said Kelly.

'Fine! Take it!' said her mom. 'I'm sure you and the girls

will get a kick out of it. But you're taking *one* suitcase – that's it! So make it work.'

Kelly flopped back on the bed and groaned through gritted teeth. Her mother got to her feet, came up to the bed and stood over her, hands on her hips. 'So, to sum it up: you're getting a lift with Antsy to the other side of the country, far away from your awful mother, so you can spend three weeks with your mates.'

'To speak Irish,' said Kelly.

Her mother raised her fists and mimicked Kelly's groan.

'And he's not "Antsy" to me,' said Kelly. 'He's just LB's dad.'

Her mother stabbed a finger in Kelly's face. 'And your mother's boss! Don't you ever forget that. Because I worry about what might happen, Kelly, if you don't respect what that man has provided for us. None of this, none of your charmed life would *be* if it wasn't for him and it wasn't for me.'

'Nice poem,' said Kelly. She looked up at her mother, eyes sparkling with defiance.

Her mom tilted her head, paused, then opened her arms and burst out laughing. 'Come here, baba. Mama's going to miss you so much.'

Their hug was a brief connect, like two moths twisting away from each other, bound for separate flames.

2

Coláiste na Carraige was five years old, founded the same year its owner, Johnny Metcalfe, was abandoned by the multi-millionaire investor who had promised him the bulk of the money he needed to transform the derelict site and its mismatch of old buildings into a luxury boutique hotel and spa.

Johnny had enough money to renovate one three-storey wing of the main building, and when he'd had the idea to open an Irish college he managed to turn some of the outbuildings into classrooms, toilets and a canteen. Until he could find a new investor, Johnny's money was made from running year-round Irish language courses that peaked in capacity during the summer with younger students in June, older students in July, and desperate students in August.

Johnny took care of the college business, and left the

language side to the retired Irish teachers he leased it to. They were the ones responsible for hiring all the staff, but Johnny was allowed to misappropriate them when needed, including his favourite from the previous summer – a diligent young student who he was now watching line up bundles of envelopes on the front desk. He moved in beside her, a pile of A4 pages clutched to his chest.

'How's my aide-de-camp?' he said, his tone cheery. 'Sounds much better in French. I'm getting all my other languages out of me before I have to speak Irish, which, effectively, involves pushing you to the forefront to speak it.'

She smiled up at him.

'First off,' Johnny continued, 'I would like to thank you for the dazzling job you did preparing the rooms for our last-minute guests. You never know what job will be thrown at you here!' He pointed to the envelopes. 'Are they the welcome packs? And your beautiful pen, ready to add our late-to-the-party names in your glorious handwriting—'

She narrowed her eyes.

'OK,' said Johnny, lowering the pages, 'trigger warning, in case there are some familiar faces here.' He put the pages down on the desk beside her. They were the last-minute application forms. She fanned them out until all five photos, clipped onto the top left-hand corner of each page, were staring up at her.

Her neck tightened, her jaw clenched.

'You can tell me all about it at a later date,' said Johnny. 'In the meantime, why don't we upgrade you to a suite? And –' he pointed to the photographs – 'I'll let you shred their faces when you're done.'

The Coláiste na Carraige minibus rattled across the cattle grid, through the towering wrought-iron entrance gates. The driver pulled up in the middle of the courtyard and yanked up the long skinny handbrake. He whipped a balled-up rain jacket out from under his seat, and a waft of stale air filled the tiny space. As he raised his arm to slide it into the sleeve, a blast of body odour followed. Rupert, sitting next to him, recoiled and turned around to the others, clinging to the back of the seat, a magnified expression of horror on his face.

The driver didn't notice. 'Stay where ye are, lads!' he said, hopping out, slamming the door behind him.

'There *is* running water in Galway? Please tell me,' said Rupert. 'Or him. Please tell him.'

'Lots of running water,' said Amber, pointing to the windscreen with her phone, which started to ping like crazy. She glanced down at her messages.

'Mother?' said Rupert.

Amber nodded, and started to fire back responses.

Lockie was staring out of the fogged-up window beside him. 'Is it going to be like this the whole time? Not that it matters. We're going nowhere. It's a prison. The guys from—'

'No stories about brain-damaged people,' said Rupert.

Amber laughed.

'We're not brain-damaged,' said Lockie.

'If you play rugby, you are. The End,' said Rupert.

'If you're a farmer, you don't even have a brain to begin with,' said Lockie.

'Yet still we produce the raw ingredients for your sandwiches,' said Rupert. He took a yellow cloth from the dashboard, turned to the foggy passenger window and wiped it down. A black SUV with tinted windows was parked by a sheltered, ivy-covered walkway. Smoke billowed from the exhaust through the red glow of the parking lights.

'LB,' said Rupert.

'And Kelly,' said Amber.

'Why didn't they give us a lift?' said Lockie, frowning.

'We wouldn't have all fit,' said Amber, quietly switching her phone to silent. 'Plus, it was last-minute and her dad's driving. And I think he's extra weird about privacy these days. Obviously, Ash works for him, so Kelly's "safe". I get it.'

Rupert put the back of his hand to his forehead. 'I'd hate to be famous, lied Rupert.'

LB was sitting beside her father in the front of the SUV as they waited for a break in the rain. She was dressed in straight-legged green combat trousers, a white T-shirt and white runners. Her black rain jacket was folded on her lap.

Kelly was watching LB's dad from the back seat. He looked nervous. Every time they'd stopped – at the shop, the petrol station, the hotel for lunch, here, now – he was checking his phone. She didn't want to ask, but she wanted to know.

'What's up?' said Kelly. 'You look . . .'

'Don't say it.'

'Antsy,' said Kelly.

'Do you have any idea how many times . . . ?' he said.

Kelly nodded. 'I do. So, what's up?'

'With me?' he said. 'Nothing. It's all good.'

'Cool, cool, cool,' said Kelly.

He smiled, but Kelly saw, in the rear-view mirror, a flash of anger in his eyes. She looked out of the window at the puddles of rain in the cracked concrete, everything grey and wet. Stir the Irish language into that and it was like the worst stew ever. Her heart pounded at the thought of not being in Roquebrune-Cap-Martin. That was her life every August. Pool, lunch, shopping, dinner, clubs. LB's family, their cool friends, LB's treasure hunts with proper prizes at the end.

She leaned into LB's dad. 'Why didn't all the rest of you still go to France?'

He reached out and gave LB's knee a pat. 'Solidarity.'

LB looked up. 'Apparently that's what made Lockie's dad freak out. If Antsy is cancelling a holiday, sh . . . tuff just got real.'

'"*Shtuff*," did it?' said Kelly.

'*You* don't curse in front of your mother,' said LB.

'I don't do anything in front of my mother,' said Kelly.

'Neither can I,' said LB's dad.

There was a hammering on the back window and everyone jumped.

'Don't move,' shouted LB's dad, throwing a protective arm across her.

'Relax!' said LB. 'We're at the Gaeltacht.'

'Open up, open up!' came a rough voice with a thick Galway accent.

LB's dad's shoulders relaxed. He hit the button for the window and it slid down.

'Can you move her up, please?' said the man outside.

'I'm trying to get the bus in . . .'

There was a pause. 'Whoa – is it yourself? I saw you in Slane in—'

LB's dad laughed. 'No. Happens all the time. No.'

'Well, you're the image of him.' The man looked into the car. 'How are ye, girls? Disgusted?'

LB laughed. Kelly ignored him.

LB's dad started the engine. 'Right. Let's get moving then.' He rolled up the window without waiting for a reply.

LB smiled at her dad. 'My brave protector.'

Kelly gave her own reflection an eye roll in the window next to her.

'Kelly's not convinced,' said LB's dad, glancing back.

Kelly gave a one-shouldered shrug. 'What?' she said. 'It was Threat Level Zero. Elderly bus man.'

'Not in the best of form?' said LB's dad, turning back to Kelly.

'I'm fine,' said Kelly.

'You'll be thankful next year,' he said. 'One less exam to worry about.'

Kelly snorted. 'Like I worry about exams.' She paused, then straightened. 'I'm thankful now, though. Already. Seriously. Totally.'

They sat in silence. Then LB's dad reached into the glovebox, took out one of his CDs and a black Sharpie.

He rolled down the window and looked out. 'Back in a minute, girls.'

He hopped out of the car, and dashed over to the minibus driver. 'Hey, do you work for Johnny?'

The driver laughed. 'I knew it was you.' He nodded. 'I'm Mick.'

LB's dad signed the CD and handed it over.

'Was that your daughter you were dropping off?'

LB's dad nodded. 'Her and her friend.'

'Well, they'll be well looked after here. Don't worry about them one bit.'

'Listen, LB – my daughter – she flies under the radar, OK? Doesn't want a lot of attention about her dad. Johnny knows the deal.'

'No, no – not a word, don't worry,' said Mick.

'Tell me security is tight,' said LB's dad.

'Ha! Is she a runner?' said Mick. 'A celebrity tearaway?'

LB's dad laughed out loud. 'Total opposite, bless her. Untouched by my crazy. But I'd keep an eye on the best friend.'

'The one with the hair? Like in the ads?'

'That's the one. Kelly Warner.'

3

Rain was pounding down on the conservatory roof and the narrow shelter that ran alongside it. Rupert, Lockie, Amber, LB and Kelly were standing side by side, wet suitcases at their feet.

'This is insane,' said Kelly. 'What is even going on here? Why has everyone else gone inside, and we're here?'

'I don't know,' said Lockie. 'The driver just said to wait here.'

'For further instructions,' said Rupert.

Lockie turned around and tried rattling the conservatory doors.

Rupert raised an imaginary bullhorn to his mouth. 'Welcome to Coláiste na Carraige! Hand over your phones, wallets...your lives.' He made beckoning gestures with his free hand. 'You heard me: hand over your best lives. And any delusions of competency in the Irish language. Come on, give them to me. Hand them over. *Máis é do thoil é*, obvs.'

'Ugh,' said Kelly. 'Irish. I'm so bad.'

Rupert held an imaginary phone. 'To upgrade from Basic Bitch Irish, press one. To hijack a minibus and return to Dublin, press two. To wish you were Réiltín Raye—'

'Oh my God – Réiltín,' said Kelly. Réiltín Raye was their classmate, a fluent Irish speaker and frequently bullied by Kelly. 'Twinkle, twinkle, little freak . . .' Réiltín was Irish for 'little star'.

'How I wonder where she is,' said Kelly, her voice flat.

'Not learning Irish,' said Amber.

Kelly glared at her, then turned her attention to Lockie, who was staring into the distance. She reached out and squeezed his bicep. She had to open her hand as wide as it could go.

'He's not an object,' said Rupert, reaching out and squeezing Lockie's other bicep.

'Get off me, you weirdos,' said Lockie, snapping back into reality, shrugging them off.

'Hate crime!' said Rupert. 'I'd like to report . . .' He trailed off, his gaze drawn towards the college. 'Oh.' He raised his Wayfarers to his forehead. 'I was wondering why it was *so* dark.'

'I was wondering why you were wearing sunglasses in the rain,' said Amber.

'Sunglasses in the rain is my spirit animal,' said Rupert. 'He was squinting at a figure standing by the first-floor window. *'In the dark blue sky you keep, and often through my curtains peep.'*

'What are you muttering?' said Lockie, irritated.

'Nothing,' said Rupert, lowering his glasses again. 'Nothing. I just—'

'Why are we still out here?' said Kelly, looking around. 'This is ridiculous. What are we even doing here? And why haven't they unlocked these doors for us? Why are there cones blocking the front?'

'Cones are for peasants,' said Lockie.

'Your dad could have dropped us at the door!' said Kelly.

'We could have been dropped at the door too!' said Lockie.

There was a sudden burst of heavier rain, and a rush of water flowed from the gutter beside them. Kelly's eyes were lit with anger. 'We should not be standing here.'

'Speaking of which . . .' said Rupert, pointing to the dark, rain-soaked college, now clearly visible.

There, at the bottom of the grey stone steps, stood Réiltín Raye, eerily still, inside an oversized rain jacket, its hood pounded by the rain, her huge, pale-green eyes stark against her skin. She was staring directly at them, a traffic cone in each hand.

Kelly's mouth dropped open. 'What the . . . ?'

Everyone exchanged glances, then watched as Réiltín turned around and walked slowly up the steps into the building, closing the double doors behind her.

'But . . .' said Kelly, 'why is *she* here? She's fluent. I don't get it.'

'Oh,' said Rupert, 'I bet she's a *cuinteoir.*'

'A what now?' said Kelly.

'An assistant,' said Rupert. 'That's what all the fluent kids do.'

They looked up as the minibus drove towards them, slowed, and stopped. Mick rolled down the window. 'Lads, did Johnny not come for ye in the jeep?'

Lockie and Rupert walked up to the bus. 'No,' said Lockie. 'Why would we need a jeep?'

'I'm very confused,' said Mick. 'I was told, drop ye where I dropped ye – Johnny, the boss, would come get ye. And ye're still here. And I'm on a mad dash to the wholesalers before closing, so I can't drop you back.'

'Back where, though?' said Rupert.

'All the way back there,' said Mick turning around and pointing. 'You're way back. At the Lodge. Beyond those trees. But there's a path you can cut through, at least.'

'This is a joke,' said Kelly.

Mick craned his neck past Lockie and Rupert, and

spotted LB and Kelly. 'Go on, so,' he said to everyone. 'Hop in. I'll drop ye.'

'Was it Johnny who sent you to the wholesalers?' said Rupert, leaning forward.

'No, no,' said Mick. 'There's no sign of Johnny.'

'Was it the *cuinteoir*?' said Rupert.

Mick nodded. ''Twas.'

'Is her name Réiltín?' said Kelly.

Mick nodded, then glanced at them in the rear-view mirror. 'Do ye know her?'

'She's in our class in Dublin,' said LB.

'Lovely girl,' said Mick.

'Who has played us like a violin,' whispered Rupert to the others as he slunk back into his seat. 'She stood at the entrance to not our building, holding two traffic cones – the same she used, in conjunction with an unsuspecting minibus driver, to guarantee we were parked/dropped/sheltered in all the wrong places and all the right weather conditions to create maximum drenchage.'

The others exchanged glances.

'I say, "Brava!",' said Rupert, giving high, silent claps.

Kelly slapped his hands hard. 'I say, "Game on."'

4

The foyer of the Lodge was circular, small and dark. Everything in it was heavy and squat, a strange mix of modern and old. LB stood alone at the centre, a green canvas army bag almost the size of her at her feet, a spotlight overhead making a halo around her blonde hair. Rupert was second to walk in, stopping dramatically, backing everyone else up, spreading Amber, Lockie and Kelly out in a single curve behind him as he took the whole scene in.

'Well, this will suck the summer right out of your veins,' said Rupert. 'Apart from our angelic centrepiece, LB.'

LB turned around and beamed.

'Such a big smile for a tiny little rosebud mouth,' said Rupert. He patted the neck of his shirt for the sunglasses he had hooked there. 'Needed to check,' he said, finding them, 'that it is, indeed, as dark as I think it is.'

Kelly laughed. 'Lockie's got his *Sunday-a.m.-where-the-hell-have-I-woken-up?* face.'

'He has woken up in glorious Galway,' said Rupert, as he stalked to the front desk and spun around, 'and the five-star – six if you include me – surroundings of Coláiste na Carraige, the spa hotel that almost was.'

The sound of curtains being whipped along a rail cut through the silence. Rupert darted back to the group, and stood clutching LB's arm. Everyone turned around to see Réiltín Raye using a wooden pole with a hook to pull back the thick red velvet curtains. When she finished, she stood where Rupert had, her face solemn, the pole straight down in front of her, clasped between her small hands.

Rupert clapped. 'Can we all give Réiltín a—'

Réiltín's eyes darted left and right. She braced herself, looked up and said: *'Caithfidh sibh labhairt as Gaeilge.' You have to talk in Irish.*

'Oh, for Christ's sake!' said Kelly, pushing past Lockie, dragging her suitcase behind her, and stopping beside Rupert. She tilted her head at Réiltín. 'Oh . . . sorry. For *Christ-íocht's sake-anna.*'

Réiltín's cheeks burned.

Lockie shot out a laugh.

Rupert placed his hands on Kelly's shoulders and gave

them a light squeeze. Then he looked at Réiltín and said, in Irish, *'Darling Kelly is very tired and doesn't know what she's saying. She doesn't even know what I'm saying.'*

A suppressed smile danced in Réiltín's eyes. Amber and LB laughed. And behind the front desk, a door burst open, and Johnny Metcalfe came through, foot first, eyes on his phone. He looked up sharply.

'Fáilte!' he said. *'Is mise* Johnny—'

'Fáilte!' said Kelly.

Johnny's head whipped towards her. 'And what are *you* welcoming *me* to, exactly?'

Kelly almost blushed.

'Only Irish word you know?' said Johnny.

Everyone laughed except Kelly, who was skewering Réiltín with a gaze, and Réiltín, who was trapped on the skewer.

Johnny pointed to Kelly. 'You – get up to speed. If I can learn enough Irish in two weeks on DuoLingo to launch a pop-up language school, you have no excuses.' He paused. 'OK – this is going to be a one-off conversation in English for m'lady.' He looked at Kelly. 'And what is m'lady's name?'

'Kelly.'

'Welcome to the Lodge,' said Johnny, addressing the group. 'I'm the boss, and Réiltín here is the uber-boss. Bypass me completely for all your needs. Breakfast is at seven a.m. Lunch you take with you from the breakfast buffet. Rustle, wrap and run. Classes start at seven forty-five. Get a two-grade bump and you get to go to the end-of-course beach party, which will be strictly alcohol-free. Do you love it?' He turned to Réiltín. 'I'm hearing gasps from the onlookers. Do we care? Don't answer that. We don't.'

He stepped forward. 'Line up, line up. Side by side where I can see you.'

Johnny carefully eyeballed each of them as he drew his gaze slowly across them. 'Don't,' he said, his face darkening, 'bring people back here. Their name is not on the list. Consider them the "crowd". Consider the trees through which you will emerge onto the campus as the "crowd barriers". Consider this backstage. And you are the Very Important People. Not that we'll be saying that out loud. Unless we want to get our privileged South Dublin heads kicked in. By privileged North Dublin heads, in fairness. I mean, the fees!' He rubbed his thumb and two fingers together.

'I'm from Kildare,' said Rupert.

Johnny nodded. 'With the poshest accent here.'

'Are you really a Southsider?' said Kelly to Johnny.

'Why do you ask?' said Johnny.

Kelly shrugged. 'Just . . . you sound like . . . someone I know from the Northside.'

Johnny gasped. 'You know someone from the Northside?'

'How old is this building?' said LB. 'What was it before?'

'This?' said Johnny, gesturing around. 'This was the main house, the hub of activity, the administrative centre. Built in the late 1800s.'

Rupert's hand shot up. 'Are there ghosts?'

Johnny paused. 'No.' He gave Réiltín a theatrical look as if to warn her not to speak.

Kelly was watching Amber. Amber's head was tilted to one side, her breath held, her fingers fidgeting at her wrist. Amber, with her long, centre-parted sandy hair to her waist, who wore boxy, baggy, boyish everything – and her delicate little bracelets. Amber caught Kelly looking and lowered her hand to her side. She gave a small smile. Kelly smiled back.

Amber raised her hand to Johnny. 'Were you joking? Are there ghosts?'

Johnny broke into a smile and shook his head. 'I'm teasing.' He paused. 'Or am I? Because ghosts choose people to appear to, don't they? For a particular reason – to finish out their lost life or atone for some prior earthly sin, or maybe to show someone the error of their ways. To stop them going down the path that led to their own demise. Early demise, in some cases.'

A skittering sound on the tiled floor broke the silence. Kelly turned to see Amber crouching down, clutching her skinny wrist. 'My bracelet! *Noo!*' Amber's hand clamped tighter on her wrist, her knuckles white, as she scanned the floor, where Rupert and LB were darting around, chasing the runaway beads of black obsidian.

Kelly rushed to her side. 'It's OK.' She turned to the others. 'No one move,' she said. 'Guys, just stop.' She spread out her arms. Everyone stopped. 'They'll stop rolling in a minute. It's not like they can roll off the edge of somewhere. We don't want to break any of them.' She looked at Lockie and mimed monster steps. She gave Amber's shoulder a reassuring squeeze. 'OK, everyone,' said Kelly. 'Carefully... carefully... pick up what's there.' She turned to Johnny. 'Do you have an envelope or something?'

Johnny stayed silent, but with a tilt of his head he guided her to Réiltín, who was already reaching behind the desk, sliding an envelope out from under a shelf. She handed it to Kelly, tentative.

Kelly gave her a big smile, turned back to the others, held out the open envelope as everyone dropped in the beads. She sealed it, and gave it to Réiltín. 'Can someone drop this into Galway for repair?'

Réiltín's eyes flicked towards Johnny. Johnny's face was a *No*.

'It's her emotional support jewellery,' said Kelly.

Amber's head jerked her way.

'You can put it on my mum's bill!' said Kelly. 'Put "Miscellaneous".'

'No,' said Amber, 'it's fine.' She reached out for the envelope and tugged it.

'I was just trying to help,' said Kelly, releasing it.

'And you did!' said Johnny. He raised his hands to regain everyone's attention. 'What I was saying was that I, personally, have never encountered a ghost anywhere on the premises. But maybe I have learned all the lessons I have to learn in this life. Or maybe because I work in high-end hospitality, where a hovering invisible presence is the highest attainable goal, I *am* the ghost.'

A long silence followed.

'So,' said Johnny, with a smile, 'what else do you need to know? What have we covered so far? Discretion. Food. Hauntings . . . Oh, yes – ultimate nightmare: hand over your phones.'

Kelly recoiled, flung a glare up at Rupert. 'Oh my God, I thought you were joking about that.'

'*I* thought I was joking,' said Rupert.

Kelly's head jerked towards Johnny. 'No one said anything about phones being handed over!'

'He did, apparently,' said Johnny, indicating Rupert.

36

'Your psychic friend.' He pointed upwards. 'My wife would love a read on her future.'

Kelly recoiled again. 'Do you *live* here?'

'Do you, like, speak in accusations?' said Johnny.

There were several sucked-in breaths.

'I have to have my phone,' said Kelly. 'For mental health reasons.'

'Not according to your mother,' said Johnny, 'who signed that life away from you, I'm afraid.' He reached out for Réiltín's clipboard. 'May I?' He took it, flipped through the pages, and nodded. 'For every guest, I see a parental betrayal in the form of a signature.'

Kelly glared at him.

'If you have a problem with the staff,' said Johnny, locking eyes with her, 'address your concerns this way.' He gestured with the clipboard to Réiltín, then handed it back to her. 'To the Box of Stolen Lives,' said Johnny, reaching down behind the front desk and pulling out a shabby grey plastic box.

'So, hold on,' said Kelly. 'This phone, which is brand new, by the way, is going to be just . . . in a random box for three weeks?'

'It's a very specific box,' said Johnny, 'and, no, they're going in the safe.'

Kelly folded her arms. 'How are we supposed to let our

parents know we arrived safely, if we don't have phones?'

Johnny sighed. 'I will be phoning all your parents as soon as you're settled into your rooms . . . and all the exit points are padlocked. Look, Kelly . . . all of you – release your phones unto Réiltín. She has no interest in them. Which is probably why she's Best in Class.' He gave a bright-eyed look in Réiltín's direction, but her eyes were on the floor. 'Right!' said Johnny. 'Room allocations! I have three keys here—'

'There are five of us,' said Kelly.

Johnny nodded. 'And four of you will be sharing. Two boys in one, two girls in the other. And one lucky loner.' He placed the keys on the front desk, each with a large carved wooden key ring and a number printed on it in white – 1, 9 and 3A.'

'Random,' said Kelly.

'So, the rooms – I could assign them, but a little birdie told me that Ms Lotus Behan likes to play games.'

LB gave little claps. 'Aww, Dad.' She looked at Johnny. 'Seriously?'

Johnny nodded.

'Aww,' said Kelly, smiling at LB. 'He did that because we're missing out on the treasure hunt this year!'

LB nodded.

Kelly turned to Johnny. 'LB does a treasure hunt every year. At their villa. In Roquebrune-Cap-Martin. In the

South of France. We go every year. Me and LB.'

'We were there once,' said Rupert, indicating the rest of them. 'Never to return.'

LB made a sad face. 'No – that's only because there's always a full house in August—'

Rupert gasped. 'Oh my God – I was teasing! That was a one-off! We knew that.' He looked at Johnny. 'It was her tenth birthday. Her dad flew us all over in the private jet. Remember—'

'The blood!' Amber blurted. Her hand shot to her mouth. Everyone stared at her. 'Oh my God. Sorry.'

'Nothing eerie there,' said Johnny. 'But thank you for sharing your story that took an unexpected turn for the darker. Like all good stories should.'

LB shook her head. 'No – it was just the housekeeper's son fell and split his head open. It was awful.'

'Poor Jeremy!' said Rupert. He gave a faux-solemn look. 'Where is he now?'

'Possibly plotting revenge,' said Johnny, 'but definitely not at the Gaeltacht.' He clapped his hands and turned to LB. 'Let the game commence!'

'Yay, Dad!' said LB.

'Yay indeed,' said Johnny, 'because this game of chance means no crying to the management if outcomes are not to your liking.' He looked around. 'Everyone game?'

39

Everyone nodded. Johnny turned to LB. 'So, what's your poison? Coin toss? Dice? Arm wrestle?'

LB smiled. 'Rock Paper Scissors.'

5

Johnny raised a finger. 'Give me a moment, because I'll be making this up as I go along.'

Everyone waited in silence.

'OK!' said Johnny. 'Here's what we're going to do.' He reached behind the desk, pulled out paper and pens, and handed them around.

'Everyone pick a room number – 1, 9 or 3A. Write it down, keep it to yourself.'

'But how do we know, if we haven't seen the rooms?' said Kelly.

'You don't!' said Johnny, flashing a smile. 'But here's what I will tell you: one is a Nice Room, one is a Very Nice Room, and one is the Penthouse, with stunning views over the water. I won't reveal which are the doubles and which is the single until required.'

Everyone wrote down their chosen number.

'If two of you pick the same number—' said Johnny.

'What if three of us do?' said Kelly.

'Cross that bridge!' said Johnny. 'If two of you pick the same number, you play Rock Paper Scissors, best of five, and winner takes the room. We'll start with LB.'

'Room 1,' said LB.

'Room 1!' said Rupert, shooting his hand up.

LB won with scissors scissors paper.

'I can confirm Room 1's a double, to be shared, obviously, with a girl.' He handed her the key. He turned to Amber and Kelly. 'And confirming neither of you picked Room 1 because you would have said so.'

'3A!' said Kelly and Amber at the same time.

'Well, now you've revealed your secret numbers,' said Johnny, 'you two can go head to head – winner gets 3A.'

'So 3A is the single room,' said Amber.

'Does that change things?' said Johnny. 'Anyone prefer not to share?'

Amber and Kelly exchanged glances. 'No, no,' they said, shaking their heads, smiling at LB.

'Then, go!' said Johnny.

Kelly won with scissors paper rock.

'Amber, you're sharing with LB,' said Johnny, 'and Kelly, I can confirm that 3A is the penthouse.'

Kelly raised her hands. 'Yaaay!' Then she turned to

Amber and made a sad face. 'But I'm sad I won't be sharing with you.'

'That's OK,' said LB. 'Yaaay, Amber!' and Amber and LB hugged. 'Have we ever shared before?' said LB.

'No,' said Amber, shaking her head.

'We did,' said Kelly pointing between herself and Amber. 'Remember? In Wexford when we were kids. And you kept doing that weird thing with your throat in the middle of the night, driving me insane.'

Amber blushed. 'I don't do it any more,' she said to LB.

'I don't mind,' said LB.

'You would if you heard it,' said Kelly, laughing. She turned to Lockie. 'Hey – Lockie didn't get to play.'

Johnny glanced at Lockie. 'I think he's OK with that. Boys, you're obviously Room 9.'

Lockie reached out for the key. 'Do you mind if I head up?'

'Oh, you're all heading up,' said Johnny. 'Now, we had a small fire in the elevator shaft and it's currently out of commission. But at least you're young and fit and all on the first floor. Apart from Ms Kelly, who is on the third floor, but you can access that at the end of the first-floor landing.' He handed her the key.

'How am I meant to get my suitcase up there?' said Kelly.

'I'll take it,' said Lockie. 'No problem.'

'Good man,' said Johnny. 'Right – Réiltín will lead the way.' He turned to her, but she was standing clutching her clipboard tight to her chest. He looked back at the others. 'Second thoughts, you're big boys and girls – you can find your own way.'

'Totally,' said Kelly, with emphasis.

Johnny scribbled directions on a piece of paper and handed them to Rupert.

'Why is it "A"?' said Kelly, looking at her key. 'Why isn't it P for penthouse?'

'That could be another game,' said Johnny. 'A is for . . . ?'

Rupert was the first up the stairs onto the first-floor landing. He studied Johnny's directions. 'Follow me!' he said, pointing right.

He stopped dead.

'Guys!' he called back. 'Our corridor is multi-coloured!'

They arrived behind him.

'And all the colours are black,' he added.

Silence descended. Rupert pointed to the carpet, walls, doors, ceiling. 'I'm seeing pitch black, raven black, Irish summer sky black . . .'

'Lockie's mood black,' said Kelly.

'Do you want to take this yourself?' Lockie said, trying

44

to hand her back her suitcase. He looked around. 'This is messed up.'

'I like it,' said Kelly, peering around. 'It reminds me of . . . my romantic history.' She flashed a smile at Lockie. He rolled his eyes.

'I think it's . . . cool,' said LB.

'I think we're all going to die,' said Amber.

Rupert cupped a hand to his ear. 'Thrive, you say?'

'Where are the lights?' said Lockie.

'Please don't be motion sensors,' said Amber looking up at the ceiling. 'They creep me out.'

Rupert took two steps forward. *Click*. A yellowy-green motion sensor light came to life overhead. He turned around to the others and hid his face in the crook of his elbow. 'Don't look at *meee*!'

The others laughed. He took advantage of the light to study Johnny's map. Behind him, the distant sound of another *click*. He spun around. Everyone stared down the corridor where a sensor light glowed, illuminating nothing.

6

Rupert used calming hands to settle everyone.

Kelly nodded down the corridor. 'The ghost of Lockie's personality.'

'Would you please just shut up?' said Lockie. 'Seriously.'

Kelly's eyes registered a sting.

'Well, this is not to scale,' said Rupert, holding Johnny's directions under the light. 'There's nothing on this to indicate a corridor so long that it leads us back to Dublin.'

'I wish,' said Kelly. She turned to LB. 'Sorry . . . it's just . . . Irish.'

'We get it,' snapped Lockie. 'We got it in first year, second year—'

'We get it,' Kelly mimicked. She reached over to her suitcase, yanked up the handle, and dragged it towards her.

'Come on,' said Lockie, walking up to Rupert. 'He drew

that in ten seconds. It looks like there's literally a T on it. How hard can it be?'

'And some Xs and not a very clear distinction between his 1 and his 9,' said Rupert. 'I've got it now. We walk down there, to Dublin, and split off, into another corridor, boys to the left, girls to the right.' He looked at Kelly with an apologetic face. 'I'm afraid he forgot to mark *which* end of the corridor is the door to 3A.'

'Yeah – "forgot",' said Lockie. He picked up his bag. Kelly kicked it as he walked away.

Amber darted in front to Rupert, hooked her arm into his.

'Everything OK?' said Rupert. He glanced down at her. She looked up at him with huge, fearful eyes. He squeezed her arm with his. 'It was not a sign,' he said, nodding down to her bare wrist.

Amber smiled up at him. 'Thanks.' She looked down the corridor. 'What motion do you think that was sensing?'

'My shadow side,' said Rupert. 'Fly, my pretty, fly. Find your spirit friends.'

Amber gave a nervous laugh.

'Stop scaring her,' said Kelly, walking behind them. She loved Amber. Amber was amazing. But Anxious Amber was like being at a funeral but no one knew who'd died. Not even Amber.

'I wasn't doing anything,' said Rupert. 'Amber's used to my ghostly ways.'

Amber glanced back at Kelly. 'I am. I just don't want to experience any.'

Kelly let out a weary breath. 'I love you, Ambs, you know I do. But you really don't make a lot of sense as a person.'

Amber squeezed Rupert's arm, gritted her teeth.

LB walked quietly behind them, head down. This was all her fault. Kelly being horrible to Lockie, Lockie hating Kelly, Amber terrified, and Rupert already deploying his calming hands. And they hadn't even got to their rooms.

First to their room were Lockie and Rupert. Lockie went straight for one of the two king-sized beds, and lay back, hands behind his head, legs crossed. Rupert did a full three-sixty at the centre of the room.

'I'm not sure what they were aiming for,' said Rupert, 'or if they even pulled the trigger.'

'It's got two beds,' said Lockie.

'So they were aiming for you,' said Rupert. 'Bravo, Johnny Owner, and your possibly mummified-in-the-attic wife.' He took in Lockie's frown. 'He pointed upwards when he mentioned his wife!' said Rupert. 'And why wasn't she there to greet us, *if she was alive*?'

Lockie laughed. 'That is definitely some English politeness rubbish.'

'Worldwide!' said Rupert. 'Etiquette! My dad thinks we have all been wired for disappointment, to automatically ask for something different, or something more. Before we even allow the first thing to settle.'

'If you settle near me tonight . . .' said Lockie. He rolled onto his side, pulling the covers with him, then stuck his head up over them and smiled.

Rupert narrowed his eyes. 'I'm wired to be deeply disappointed with whatever you have to offer.'

Réiltín sat cross-legged at the centre of her queen-sized bed, dressed in a navy tank top and matching shorts, leaning over her clipboard, her arms toned, her thick hair piled into a topknot. Even seeing Kelly Warner's name tightened her chest. She was constantly braced for Kelly's smirks and overlong looks and glances flashed at whomever she wanted to turn against her. Who could she turn against her here? Not Johnny. She knew Johnny liked her. And he actually paid attention to her. He had recognised the name of her school when he saw it on the others' applications. And even though she had never said anything to him about being bullied back in Dublin, he clearly picked up on how happy she was to be away. Réiltín knew she'd originally got the job through a friend of her mom's, so she worked extra hard to prove she deserved it. And she wasn't going to screw that up because of Kelly Warner.

Knowing she was coming back to the Gaeltacht was the only thing that got Réiltín through fifth year. She was expecting the same summer she had last year, and with the best friend she had ever made. They had met on their first day the previous June, when they were both *cuinteoirs* for the younger kids. And in August, they both switched to working for Johnny. She felt like a completely different person with him. Her real self. She had never talked to her new friend about Kelly and the others – he thought she was fierce and she didn't want to change that. Because allowing someone to bully her didn't feel very fierce— She stopped . . . Well, not *allowing* her. Just doing everything she possibly could to avoid her. Like spending her summer three hundred kilometres away, in the last place on earth she thought *she* would ever turn up. And in a cruel twist her best friend was the one three hundred kilometres away.

Réiltín felt a stab of anger. She jumped up, stormed across the floor into the bathroom, slammed the door and screamed. Thank you, Johnny, for your soundproofing. And your scissors. She grabbed them from the shelf above the sink, beside the one photo she hadn't shredded. She went over to the toilet, stood over it, and cut Kelly Warner's paper face into tiny pieces. Why shred when you could go snip by satisfying snip?

7

Amber stood in the en suite bathroom of Room 1, head bowed, clutching the sink.

Black obsidian beads scattering—

Bony fingers darting out from under the skirting boards—

Stop.

. . . desperately clawing at them, pulling them down into a gloomy underworld.

Amber sucked in a huge breath. She looked at herself in the mirror. *Stop!* She steadied her gaze, and started to count the seconds of her breaths until her breathing settled. She turned on the cold tap, and took the envelope off the shelf in front of her. She shook the beads into her hand, and held them carefully under the cool water, then laid them out on a facecloth to dry. She looked around the bathroom. It was beautiful. So was the bedroom. It had to be the Very Nice Room. But she still wanted 3A. It wasn't like she knew it was the penthouse when she'd written it down. She just had a good feeling about it. She finished drying the beads, put them into her pocket and exhaled slowly. She walked back out and saw LB kneeling on the floor at her open bag. Kelly was sitting on the dressing table.

'Regal, bitchanna,' said Kelly, looking around. 'Luxe.' She paused. 'I'll miss you in the penthouse, though. Who's getting which bed?'

'I'll take the single,' said Amber.

'Are you sure?' said LB, pausing, looking up at her. 'We could toss a coin.'

'No – I'm sure,' said Amber. 'Seriously. I actually like single beds. I sleep in a single bed, remember.'

'Oh yeah,' said LB. 'But that one's rammed up against the wall.'

'It's cosy,' said Amber.

'OK,' said LB, standing up, holding her soap bag, about to head to the bathroom.

'Wait,' said Kelly. 'Come with me – check out the penthouse. Don't be bitter.'

LB laughed. 'I'm wrecked.'

'Me too,' said Amber. 'And I have to unpack.'

'Me too,' said LB.

Kelly rolled her eyes. 'Fine, then! Enjoy your period-drama-four-poster-thwarted-love affair.'

Amber rubbed a hand down LB's arm. LB wrapped her leg around Amber's. 'Who said anything about thwarted?' said Amber.

As soon as LB went into the bathroom, Amber opened her suitcase and pulled out a dark navy box with a glowing moon at the centre: LA LUNA ORACLE DECK. She pulled off the lid, took out the cards, and held them between her hands, holding them until her shoulders relaxed. She let out a long, relieved breath. She closed her eyes, and said, 'Tell me what I need to know right now.' She started to shuffle the cards when the bathroom door swung open and LB walked out. Amber reached for the box, and pulled it towards her.

'Ooh!' said LB. 'You brought your cards. You must give me a reading before we go.'

'I will,' said Amber, her eyes lighting up.

'Do you bring them everywhere?' said LB, curious.

'Not *everywhere*,' said Amber.

'Like, not into the bathroom,' said LB, doing an impression of her darting in.

Amber laughed. She put the cards back in the box, and put them in the bottom drawer of her bedside cabinet. She really did want to bring the deck into the bathroom, find out something that would make her feel better, but there was no point – she didn't have her phone or any other light. She suddenly realised she was sharing a room. They had all just assumed they were getting their own rooms. That meant that the chances of her being able to do her bedtime oracle card reading or her morning reading without LB being around were really slim. But she might get away with the lunchtime ones. And she could always get up earlier, when LB was out for her run. Maybe that's why she'd been so drawn to 3A – some part of her knew it was a single room. And she could do all the readings she wanted without having to worry.

Kelly stood at the open door to 3A. A narrow flight of steep wooden stairs rose directly in front of her in the gloom.

'OK, what?' She left her suitcase where it was and stepped over the threshold to the bottom of the steps, then felt around the wall for a light switch. There was none. But as soon as she took two steps up, another yellowy motion sensor light came on. She slowly climbed the stairs. Moonlight shone faintly through an arched window, pooling on the floorboards. Kelly's head jerked right, her gaze travelling along a line of wrought-iron beds, every one of them made up with all-white bedlinen. On each bed, there was a white scalloped-edge bedspread, a single cushion with a white crocheted cover, and a beige wool blanket folded at the end. On the wall behind every bed hung a framed pressed flower.

Kelly turned around and stared blankly at the painting on the wall opposite her featuring a sad girl with a sad dog under a weeping willow. Why? Just . . . why? Her heart lurched at the thought of three weeks going up and down those stairs, going to sleep in one of those beds, waking up in it, probably with nightmares, and just the trapped panic and the not-supposed-to-be-complaining because: mom's boss and LB's dad and favours and fees and being grateful and—

Something crawled across her arm, spidery and light. Kelly screamed. And ran.

8

Rupert gasped. 'A is for Attic!' He held up the key triumphantly. Kelly, hovering on the steps behind him, nudged him forward out of her way and snatched the key from his hand as she passed. Rupert was dressed in cotton white-and-whiter striped pyjamas, a pale blue eye mask holding back his hair, which was being warmed by the swinging bulb of an overhead light as he idly pushed the chain back and forth. He looked around in the searing brightness.

'What in the eerie landscape of yore is this?' he said, stepping aside to let Lockie through.

Lockie tried to turn his snort of laughter into a cough.

'It's not funny,' said Kelly, sitting down on the bed, glowering at him. 'What even is this?'

'Well, it's called a dormitory,' said Rupert. 'It's where—'

'Shut up,' said Kelly.

'Spiders!' said Lockie, giving Rupert a hurry-up gesture.

'We're not squishing them,' said Rupert. 'We will set them free.'

He and Lockie did a thorough check of the room, and reconvened in front of Kelly.

'Clear,' said Rupert. 'Apart from the mummified wife.'

Kelly shuddered. 'I mean . . . why even is this a room? Like, is this place not supposed to be, or will be, a five-star hotel? What was it before? An orphanage?'

'He skipped over that question, did you notice? said Rupert. 'A home for wayward teens? Who knows? Strikes me that Johnny Owner is a font of whatever the occasion requires. As long as he can make money from it. You have a daughter who needs to learn Irish? I have just the Gaeltacht for you! Five-star accommodation, you say?' And he literally runs around with rolls of carpet and wallpaper and . . . obviously he ran out of steam before he made it up here.'

'I wish we could google him,' said Kelly, eyes narrowed.

'Johnny?' said Lockie. 'Why? So you can what? Tell us something awful you found out about him?'

Kelly stared at him. 'What? No.'

'Why, then?' said Lockie.

'I'm just interested,' said Kelly.

She leaned out, tugged at Lockie's sleeve and pouted

up at him. He sat down beside her and gave Rupert a look of gentle pleading.

'OK, my pretty,' said Rupert to Kelly. 'Not to hurry things along, but what is it we can do for you? Were we just here for the imaginary spiders?'

'Yes,' said Kelly. 'No. I . . .' She sat up.

'She wants to swap rooms,' said Lockie, leaning back to take a look at her.

'No, I don't!' said Kelly.

'She does,' said Lockie. 'She's got her face.' He mimicked her sad eyes and pout.

She elbowed him.

'So what is it, then?' said Rupert. 'Fear? Of spiders? Fear of rooms with multiple beds? Fear of nothing but allergy to simple living?' He paused. 'If you're actually afraid, I'll stay here tonight. One-time offer, because have you seen my bed?'

'I don't want to see any more beds,' said Kelly. 'There's just something about being in a room with seven empty beds . . .'

' . . . that makes you feel like Snow White?' said Rupert. 'And the lads are away on a stag?'

Lockie snorted a laugh. 'Snow White. Yeah.'

Kelly's eyes flashed with anger. She kicked out, and caught the underside of Lockie's foot with her runner.

'Calm down, Kel,' said Lockie. 'What's with the kicking? I was only—'

Rupert turned to Kelly. 'What about the girls? Could you stay in their room?'

'Yeah – why didn't you wake *them* up?' said Lockie.

'I thought it was spiders,' said Kelly.

Lockie stood up, stretched and yawned. 'Right – are you going to be a big girl, or are we escorting you back to wake the others up? You're not staying in our room.'

Kelly glared at him, then flashed a smile. 'I'm fine. Just go, OK?'

Johnny stood under an oak tree, a cigarette in his hand, looking up at the shadows crossing the arched attic window. He smiled. The game was fun. Poor Antsy was trying to get the whole thing off to a cheery start. Johnny took a deep drag on his cigarette and held his breath. *And poor little LB, innocent and bright-eyed. I hope you stay that way, regardless of what's coming down the line.* Smoke shot through his lips. *But I won't hold my breath.*

Hours later, Amber jolted awake to a sound, like a low moan, coming from somewhere on the corridor outside. She was lying on her back and turned slowly to her right where she saw LB sleeping. She heard the sound again, a different type of moan. Her heart started to pound. She didn't want to get up, but she didn't want to stay freaking out about it if it was nothing. She pushed back the covers, slipped out of bed, and went to the door. She looked out, but it was pitch dark. Her shoulders slumped. Sensor lights. She didn't want to go out. She began looking around for something to stick under the one that was closest, but after a moment she wedged the door open and darted out. The light sensor clicked on, briefly flickering, and her eye caught, down the corridor, something shadowy and black sweep out of a room, pause, then sweep back in again as a door rattled.

It all happened so quickly that, in the hesitant light, she couldn't be sure she hadn't hallucinated it.

9

Rupert stood at the breakfast buffet dressed in a pale-pink V-neck T-shirt with a white round-neck T-shirt underneath, black straight-leg jeans and brown loafers. He took a bowl and reached for the long handle of a silver serving spoon sticking out of the fruit salad.

'Morning, Most Handsome,' said LB, appearing beside him.

'Morning, Most Joyful,' said Rupert. He took in her red cheeks, her hair down and wet. 'Did you go for a run already?'

She nodded. 'Have you seen the beach?' She reached for a bowl.

'How did you sleep?' said Rupert. 'Anyone break your door down?'

'What?' said LB.

'Kelly,' said Rupert. 'In the penthouse with the daggers.'

Amber, hair wrapped in one fluffy white towel, body wrapped in another, hauled her rucksack up onto the bed and took out a long-sleeved beige top, matching beige trousers and a pair of black boots. She got dressed, brushed her wet hair, and went back over to her bed. She pulled out the bottom drawer of the bedside cabinet, took out one of her oracle decks, and started to shuffle.

Kelly woke with a start. She lay very still, waiting for the pounding in her chest to stop. She couldn't remember the nightmare, and couldn't remember the last time she'd had one. She was about to reach out for her phone, then groaned. The sound of screeching birds erupted outside her window.

'Oh my God. Birds! Shut. Up.'

She slammed her head back onto the pillow. When she rolled over, pulling the covers with her, she saw the grim line of vacant beds, and caught the numbers on the alarm clock: 07:15.

She slapped the covers hard. She heard a scratching sound at the window, and turned to see two white and grey herring gulls pecking on the ledge.

'No way,' she said. 'No way. No way. No way.'

She scrambled out of the bed on the opposite side.

I AM STILL IN THE NIGHTMARE.

Amber walked into the dining room and saw Rupert standing at the juice dispenser, moving his glass back and forth to mix orange and grapefruit juice.

'Claire Standish, *The Breakfast Club*,' blurted Amber as she walked towards him.

'Correct!' said Rupert.

LB slapped his arm when he sat back down at the table. 'That wasn't fair! You didn't say you were a girl.'

'Hate crime!' said Rupert. 'Were you trying to guess?'

'Of course I was,' said LB. 'I'm always trying to guess things.'

'Guess how much Kelly loved her room last night,' said Amber.

'I filled her in,' said Rupert.

'Well, here's part two of the story. I just met her on the way to "talk to the management".'

'Oh dear,' said Rupert. 'We all know what's going to happen there.'

Johnny sat sideways at his desk, his feet up on a cardboard box beside it, his fingers steepled, staring at Kelly as she finished speaking. Then he lowered his index finger onto a list of rules, in English, that had been sent to the parents and, specifically, to the part that said, 'must, for the duration of their stay, speak in Irish at all times'. Then he picked up a red Sharpie and underlined it. Then he underlined the rest of the sentence twice: '<u>or risk expulsion</u>*'. Then he circled the asterisk and the matching one at the bottom of the page next to the tiny print that said: 'No refunds.' Then he drew an exclamation mark. Then he added another one. Then he pointed to his office door.

'Oh, hold on,' he said, taking his feet off the cardboard box and sitting up. 'I'll walk you back.'

'I thought we had to talk in Irish,' said Kelly. 'And I'm fine.'

Johnny was pulling open the cardboard box. 'No, you're not. You're helping me.' He took out the top package – black, wrapped in clear plastic with an 'XL' on a round sticker in the bottom corner. He searched through the rest of them.

'How do you say, "One size fits all" in Irish?' he said. 'Rhetorical question.' He ripped open the package and pulled out a black hoodie, holding it up by the shoulders and shaking it out. Across the back, in gold foil cursive, was written *Coláiste na Carraige*.

'Nice,' he said, hanging it on the arm of the chair. '*Very* nice *indeed.*'

He threw two packages at Kelly, took a pile himself, and

pointed to the door again. He followed her out, throwing a package onto the front desk as he walked past.

They arrived at the dining room, and handed out the hoodies to Rupert, Amber and LB who were just finishing breakfast.

'Where's the big guy?' Johnny said.

'In his room,' said Rupert, as Kelly sat down beside him.

'Take his for him,' said Johnny. He scanned the table. 'Did he eat? I don't want anyone to think we're not feeding you.'

'He hasn't come down yet,' said Rupert.

'Before I go,' said Johnny, 'the only thing I ask of you all is that you wear these on the beach on the last night. For the promo shot.'

'What if we don't qualify for the beach party?' said Kelly.

'High hopes here,' said Johnny. 'Everyone qualifies for the promo shot.'

Kelly gave her one-shoulder shrug.

'You know it's a badge of honour to survive this course,' said Johnny.

'What if you don't survive?' said Kelly.

'If I don't,' said Rupert, holding up his hoodie after Johnny had walked away, 'please don't let this be the crime scene in which my body is found.'

* * *

Lockie lay in bed, staring at the ceiling. Tears welled in his eyes. He swiped them away with an angry hand. He looked at the clock. 07:18. And now he had twelve minutes to get up, get ready and get out. He didn't want to eat. His stomach felt hollowed out. If he knew this was what it was like when you broke up with someone you loved, he never would have fallen in love in the first place. That was one of the main lies he had tried out. He wished he'd never met Clare. That was another. He finally understood the songs he used to skip. Hearing song lyrics was like being stealth-bombed into tears that could happen anywhere, any time. Last night, Rupert had figured out the ancient radio alarm clock and they were blasted awake earlier by some guy singing about his girlfriend breaking up with him.

But Lockie's wasn't a break-up. It was a controlled explosion. With a Clare's-dad-shaped silhouette laughing in the blast. Lockie sucked in a huge breath and held it as he pictured punching that silhouette down, down, down, until it was a flat line.

'Asshole,' he said, whipping off the covers, and landing his feet hard on the velvety carpet. He paused, then rubbed them back and forth on the soothing velvet. He stood up. 'Thank you –' He walked towards the bathroom – 'I said to a carpet.' He shook his head. 'This is how people lose their mind.'

He paused in front of a long mirror, his blond hair askew, his eyes swollen, the waistband of his white boxers a little rippled, his ribs a little more pronounced. Then his head went straight to Clare, and how she would stand in front of him, tiny, pulling his arms around her, lying back against him as he kissed the top of her head, and then they would look at each other in the reflection and know they looked perfect together and one of them would always say it out loud, but both of them would always know that that had never mattered. Being perfect together, feeling perfect together was the best thing he had ever known. Tears slid down his face again.

Her father was an asshole. His father was an asshole. And all he wanted to do was love the girl he loved.

10

THREE WEEKS LATER

Lockie stood swaying on the beach. He wasn't supposed to be there. He couldn't find the others. He looked around, desperate to settle his vision on something that made sense. Flames shot up from the dying bonfire and sparks exploded like fireworks. The scattered groups around it cheered.

'Throw more on,' someone shouted.

Lockie staggered forward and blinked. There was a sea of hoodies that looked like everyone's backs were on fire. He blinked again and got momentary focus. He needed water. He wandered over to the food truck. It was closed. He started to walk around the back of it when he heard Johnny's voice.

'Give me the bottle!' Johnny was saying. 'Now!'

Lockie could hear sobbing.

'What are you like?' said Johnny. 'Drunkest girl on the

beach! Was that what you were aiming for?'

Lockie leaned out and squinted into the low light. Something looked like it was floating in front of gold ribbons hovering over two lollipop sticks. He blinked and saw the college hoodie, and legs and, for a moment, a flash of skin from inside the hood.

'Stop looking around for someone to rescue you!' snapped Johnny.

Lockie jerked back in, pressing himself against the side of the truck, squeezing his eyes shut.

No drinking. Stay out of trouble. Stay away from girls.

'Grow up!' shouted Johnny. 'Have you not got it yet? No one is coming to rescue you. No one even knows you're here!'

1 1

After breakfast, Amber, Rupert, Kelly and LB walked down the sloping grass from the Lodge.

'Johnny is so unprofessional,' said Kelly. 'Like, if parents knew what he was like—'

Amber laughed. 'Parents are looking at the man, just . . . "Thank you, thank you, thank you!"'

LB nodded. 'And they're knocking back champagne and drawing smiley faces on the calendar.'

'My mom definitely is,' said Kelly.

'No she's not,' said LB. 'She's too busy standing over Dad with a whip. "Write more songs, make more money, make more money!"'

Kelly laughed. 'And your dad's like, "I can't, I *caaan't*."'

LB laughed. 'And your mom's like, "My daughter has needs!" In Brown Thomas. In a size five.'

71

Rupert led the way through the gap in the trees that led onto the campus.

'You expect something magical on the other side,' said Rupert, 'and you get this.' He gestured down to a long single-storey flat-roofed building, two classrooms wide. On the grass in front of it there was a row of picnic tables with benches. Some of the students sitting outside the classroom glanced up.

'We're like those tribes who emerge from the trees to confront interlopers,' said Rupert.

'We're not here to make friends,' said Amber in a movie-hero voice.

'We brought our own,' said LB.

'And already lost one of them,' said Amber.

'No,' said Rupert, looking behind them to where Lockie was squeezing through the gap in the trees.

'This whole thing is nuts,' said Lockie. 'I feel like . . . it feels like we're in an alternate universe. One minute I'm in Dublin, next thing I'm climbing through trees—'

'Oh my God, shut up everyone!' said LB. 'Shut up! Stop making me feel like crap.'

'No one's making you feel like crap,' said Kelly.

'You are!' said LB. 'Apart from Amber.' She turned to her. 'But I can tell you're freaking out.'

'No, I'm not,' said Amber.

72

'OK – fine,' said LB. 'My point is, you know none of us would be here if Dad hadn't pulled strings. And he wouldn't have done that if it wasn't because of me.'

'LB,' said Rupert, 'none of our parents were *forced* to send us. We're here because they *voluntarily* forced us.'

'But there wouldn't have *been* any place to send us, is my point,' said LB, 'if he hadn't got us in here at the last minute. And this is, like, a nice thing he did.' She shrugged. 'And you're all just moaning non-stop. Apart from Amber and Rupert.'

'So, just me and Lockie,' said Kelly. 'Thanks.'

Lockie shot Kelly a look. 'Yes, just us!'

Kelly matched his look. 'It's not my fault—'

'No!' said Lockie. 'It never is!'

'Oh my God, seriously,' said LB, storming down the slope.

'Nice one, Lockie,' said Kelly, pushing past him and running after LB.

The Irish teacher, pretty and bright-eyed, with red corkscrew curls to her shoulders, was sitting at the edge of her desk at the top of the classroom, nodding and smiling as everyone walked in. She gave an extra ten minutes to allow for stragglers, then stood up.

'*Miss Breathnach is ainm dom*,' she said. '*Fáilte go Coláiste na Carraige*.' She looked around the classroom at the miserable faces. 'Or should I say "hell"?'

Everyone laughed.

'We love her,' mouthed Rupert to the others. They all nodded. 'Mouthing in English doesn't count,' he added.

Kelly listened for a while at the beginning of class, understanding some of the obvious words, but then zoned out. She couldn't make sense of any sentences spoken at high speed by a native speaker, even one who made Irish sound way nicer than anyone else she'd heard. Ugh, though. She was still going to fail. She looked around the room, wishing she could have someone else's brain. Her eyes fell upon a pale guy in a sports jersey, skinny shoulders hunched to his ears, jaw clenching and unclenching . . . *Not that freak's, though*. He caught her eye and smiled. Of course he did. Kelly gave him a tight smile back. Just in case he was a psycho. Or knew someone hot.

Amber's pen hovered over a mostly blank page. It was an introductory class; she was beyond this level, but right now, she really wished it was advanced enough that she could be focused on the teacher instead of this *weight*. Instead of being pulled around the classroom, looking for someone else who was feeling what she was feeling. It was as if, when she walked through the classroom door, she had stepped through a portal and an invisible cloak of negative energy had been dropped onto her shoulders and she couldn't shake it off. She shifted in her seat, shook out her arm, and refocused on Irish. Of all the six subjects she was doing for her Leaving, Irish was the one she pretty much knew she'd get a H1 in. She already got H2s, and sixth year would have bumped her up, anyway. These three weeks, she knew, were her mother's insurance policy. Her mother always needed insurance. And spare wheels. And life jackets on dry land. Amber stopped breathing, and then she noticed. She put her hand to her chest and pressed against it, as if to remind it how it was meant to move, to remind herself to just . . . *breathe and let things be*. She looked over at beautiful Rupert, her circuit breaker to the spirals of doom which her mother managed to draw her into. Even when she wasn't around.

12

At lunch, Kelly sat slumped on top of the picnic table that LB, Amber and Rupert were eating at, her feet on the bench beside Rupert.

'So,' said Rupert, 'I have spotted three Boys for Kelly...'

'Shut up,' said Kelly. Then: 'Did you get their numbers?'

'No, but I counted their tattoos,' said Rupert, 'and they had nine hundred between them.'

'Where is Lockie?' said Kelly, irritated.

'You're so mean sending him in to queue,' said LB.

'I didn't send him in!' said Kelly. 'He offered.'

'To put himself out of your misery,' said Rupert.

'I just wanted some crisps,' said Kelly.

'You're still treating him like you're together,' said LB.

'No,' said Amber, shaking her head. 'Actually, he's *allowing* her to do that.'

'Thank you!' said Kelly. She turned to LB. 'And stop

saying Lockie and I were "together" like we were actually . . . together.'

'Oh my God – you were!' said LB.

'We hooked up a few times,' said Kelly, shrugging.

Everyone exchanged glances.

'Oh my God – a million times!' said LB. 'Now you're just . . .'

'Erasing him from her romantic history,' said Rupert.

'Why don't they have crisps in the Lodge?' said Kelly.

'I don't know,' said Rupert. 'Why don't they have normal lighting and short corridors?'

'Crisps are cheaper,' said Kelly. 'And they could make money on them.'

Rupert looked at her. 'Maybe you could complain to the management.'

'He's such an asshole – Johnny,' said Kelly. 'He told me to talk to Réiltín about my room. Knowing I actually can't. What's the Irish for "creepy shithole with angry birds"?'

'I'll swap with you,' said Amber.

'Where the hell is Lockie?' said Kelly. She paused and turned to Amber. 'What did you just say?'

'I'll swap with you.' She turned to LB. 'If that's OK with you.'

LB nodded. 'Of course it is.'

Rupert laid a gentle hand on Amber's arm. 'You might want to see the room in question first.'

'She might not!' said Kelly. 'I vote for not!'

Amber laughed. 'I don't mind. Seriously. I'll swap.'

'Will this end the complaints?' said LB to Kelly, pushing herself up from the table.

Lockie was sitting alone at a table in the canteen, staring into space, two packets of crisps in front of him, his hands cupped around them.

'Hey,' said LB, walking up. 'What's up?'

'Oh, sorry,' he said, handing her the crisps.

'No,' said LB, sitting down beside him. 'What's going on? I saw you through the window.'

Lockie put his head in his hands.

'You can tell me,' said LB, laying her hands over his.

He let out a breath. 'It's over with me and Clare.'

'What?' said LB. 'No way! You guys are obsessed.'

'Her dad found texts.' He gave her a meaningful look.

'Oh.'

'And went mental,' said Lockie. 'But I didn't send them. She's pretty much the only girl I *haven't* sent photos to . . . like that. Kelly and I were always sending stuff to each other.' He paused. 'Sorry.'

'No, I know. It's fine.'

'Me and Clare never did. Her dad's so strict. So I'm like, why is he lying about photos? Using that as an excuse to break us up? That's messed up.' He paused. 'I know the others think I'm being a weirdo, but I don't want to get into it. Will you just tell them?'

'You're not being a weirdo,' said LB.

'Thanks,' said Lockie.

He turned to her. 'Do you think . . . What if the photos are from another guy?'

'No way,' said LB. 'Clare's mad about you. She's so not like that.'

Lockie let out a breath. 'What am I supposed to do?'

'Nothing for now,' said LB. 'But . . . her dad can't control her forever.'

'So I'm just supposed to wait?' said Lockie.

'Maybe, if that's what it takes,' said LB.

Kelly twisted around on the bench, first looking for Lockie, then idly scanning the crowd of students.

'Does everyone hate us, do you think?'

'What? Why?' said Amber.

'Because they're in random bunk beds eating stew and we're . . .' Kelly shrugged.

'Backstage?' said Amber.

'Very Important People?' said Rupert. 'I don't think that

news has reached the masses. Maybe Miss Breathnach could do an after-class reveal.'

It turned out that Miss Breathnach did do an after-class reveal, starting with Irish that most of them understood – does anyone know the English for Carraig na nGealt, the rock that inspired the college name. Nobody did.

She smiled. 'In English – the Rock of Lunatics.'

Everyone laughed. She reverted to Irish, and Amber translated the essence of it for the others.

'It's called that,' said Amber, her voice low, 'because hundreds of years ago, that's where "lunatics" went on a kind of pilgrimage, because there's a holy well on top that was supposed to heal them.'

'Not sure the top of a – what? – hundred-foot-high rock is the best place for the loons to gather,' whispered Rupert.

They all turned back to Miss Breathnach, who was gesturing beyond the window in the direction of the Lodge.

'Here's your backstage VIP announcement,' said Rupert to Kelly.

Kelly nodded, a little proud, expectant.

Miss Breathnach spoke again, and they all understood 'trees' and 'the other side of them'.

Rupert looked at Amber and whispered, 'What was that last bit?'

LB understood some of it. 'Something about building and the late 1800s.'

Everyone looked at Amber, who turned, wide-eyed, towards them. 'She said, "Where better than in the shadow of the Rock of Lunatics to *build an asylum*"!'

13

Amber stood in the attic room, carefully settling the selenite sphere on its stand on top of the chest of drawers. She rearranged the crystals beside it. She took her lighter and lit a sage smudge stick and, holding a bowl under it, wafted the smoke around the room before stubbing it out. She sat down on the bed by the window. She smiled as she looked around the room, then felt guilt swell like a wave inside her. She felt saner in an asylum than she did at home. She felt happier without her phone, calmer for not being reachable, for not being responsible for her mother's fears, for not having to confirm that she was alive or eating or breathing or not hurting herself. Even though she knew that going to the Gaeltacht was part of her mother's back-up plan in case the new Irish teacher was rubbish, she still didn't think it would override her mother's need for her to be around. Thank God for Rupe's dad, who sold her on the idea. And her mom knew Amber would always be safe with Rupert. Plus, if a seventy-two-year-old farmer could cope without his son for three weeks, her forty-one-year-old mother could too. Amber stood up and moved towards the stairs. She paused at the stubbed-out smudge stick and walked on. Halfway down the stairs, she ran back up, plucked it out of the bowl, went to the bathroom and ran the charred black top under the tap.

Everyone was sitting at the table when Amber arrived, all looking at Rupert, who was carefully unfolding a yellowed piece of paper. She sat opposite him.

'Where did you get that?' said Kelly.

'Not to be teacher's pet,' said Rupert, 'but I did approach her after class, having noticed the glee in her eye when discussing Carraig na nGealt. I correctly guessed that she had a particular interest in it. And I said we did as well, because we now expected to be murdered in our beds in the Lodge. No, I didn't. But she did give me this to show you.'

He turned the page around. It was a sketch of a building with printed columns of text underneath.

'The *before* shot,' said Rupert. 'As in . . . the Lodge. Though, with some structural changes.' He turned it back to himself and squinted at the text underneath. 'A little history to not reassure us on any level?'

He began to read out loud:

'The small village of Carricknagalt was named after Carraig na nGealt – the Rock of Lunatics, so called as it was where those found to be afflicted with a "turbulence of the mind" . . .'

He paused. 'No offence to the reader.' And pointed to himself. He continued reading:

' . . . for "stagnancy of the spirit"—'

'No offence to Lockie,' said Kelly.

' . . . were sent, due to the healing properties of its well-water, known to soothe the souls of even the most feral. (No offence to Kelly.) *The rock, which stands ninety-eight foot high, sits just three hundred feet from the shore and is, in fact, a tidal island. Stone steps, chiselled into the rock, wind their way up to the grassy peak on which its healing well stands. In later years, where better to build an asylum, than on the land from which this imposing monolith extends?*

The causeway, exposed at low tide, leads those who cross it to its rocky foreshore, which is not, in fact, made of rocks but of the tiny phalanges of patients whose minds were so turbulent, they couldn't follow the directions to the well. But died trying.'

Silence.

Rupert turned around. 'Oh my God – I made the last bit up.'

After dinner, everyone gathered in Amber's room, and looked out of the window to Carraig na nGealt.

'So,' said LB. 'It's got steps . . .' She smiled, eyes bright.

'"Chiselled" steps,' said Rupert. 'Hands down who here has confidence in a chiselled step?'

'You could climb it without any steps,' said LB. 'Fifteen minutes, max. It's just . . . a hike with extra help.'

'And what are you going to do – swim there?' said Kelly.

'You misunderstood,' said Rupert. 'She's not going near it.'

'It's a tidal island,' said LB. 'Rupert just said – you can walk across the causeway at low tide. Three hundred feet? Five minutes.'

Kelly sniffed the air, and turned to Amber. 'I'm really offended that you saged the place after I left.' She gestured around the room. 'But I like what you've done to it.'

'Thank you,' said Amber. 'And I sage everywhere. It was nothing to do with you.'

Lockie looked at LB. 'I'd be up for climbing that, if you're going.'

'Climbing that,' said Rupert, pointing to the top, 'would be the height of lunacy.'

Kelly nodded. 'Like looking out a window in August and not seeing Monaco.'

LB and Lockie left Amber's room together.

'I'll walk you to your room,' said Lockie.

'I'll walk you to yours,' said LB. 'Tuck you in before Rupe keeps you awake with ghost stories.'

Lockie smiled. 'You didn't tell the others about Clare . . .'

'Not yet,' said LB. 'Thought I'd buy you some time . . .'

He looked at her. 'From Kelly, you mean . . .'

'I didn't say that,' said LB. 'It's just – the humour she's in . . . she could come out with anything. Not on purpose.'

'I can't get it out of my head . . . Clare, her dad . . .' He paused. 'He thinks all I do is play rugby, watch rugby and drink.'

They exchanged glances.

Lockie laughed. 'Fair enough. But he actually said to her, "Marcus Loughnane won't end up going to college.

He'll end up in some dead-end job—"'

'And what?' said LB. 'Not provide for her and the kids?'

Lockie laughed. 'He does think I'm thick, though. Actually, he thinks the exact same as my dad.'

'Oh my God,' said LB, 'your dad doesn't think that.'

Lockie nodded. 'He does.' He ran his fingers through his hair, ruffling it, leaving it messy. LB felt a wash of sadness come over her. That was how she remembered Lockie when he was a kid. His mother used to drop him off at piano on Saturdays, and kiss him on the cheek, and mess up his hair just like that, and he always let her. He never ducked away. LB remembered thinking how unusual that was – how special. It was like he knew.

'If your dad doesn't believe in you,' said LB, 'two things. One: do you think your mother would have?'

'Yes – totally,' said Lockie.

'No hesitation, so that's good,' said LB. 'And second thing – *I* believe in you. I believe you can be anything you want to be. I'm not being an internet quote. It's the truth.'

Later that night, Rupert's eyes sprung open, his eyelashes catching on his eye mask. He dragged it off.

'Lockie!' he hissed, turning towards him. 'Wake up . . . oh.'

Rupert followed the glow of a dim light halfway down the room to discover Lockie sitting at his desk, headphones on, writing.

'So, no, is the answer,' said Rupert. 'You did not hear whatever the haunted house of horrors hell was just happening.'

He rolled onto his back, relieved in the silence. The moaning started again. Rupert's arms slapped the covers. Lockie turned when he caught the movement, and pulled off his headphones.

'OK,' said Rupert, 'I'm being haunted over here. So we need to address this.' He could see Lockie's Irish book and notes on the desk. 'And now a second shock,' said Rupert. 'Is there nowhere I can turn?'

'What are you talking about – haunted?' said Lockie.

'I'm talking about that!' said Rupert, pointing in the direction of his bed, then all around the room. 'That . . .' Everything was silent. He gave it another thirty seconds. 'Fine!' he said. 'As you were.'

14

Rupert pressed his hands slowly down on the table at breakfast and looked around at the others.

'OK, so let me get this straight,' he said, '*all* of us, except Lockie and LB, have heard something in the middle of the night? And no one said anything.'

'Until now,' said Kelly.

'So everyone was waiting for someone else to say it out loud,' said Rupert. He looked around. 'Have you all been going around quietly disturbed?'

'No more than usual,' said Amber.

LB raised her hand. 'Actually, I heard something the first night.'

'It's not a competition,' said Kelly.

LB turned to Amber. 'Remember I went into the bathroom and came right back out again? I was in there and I heard this, like, muffled scream.'

'What? Why didn't you say anything?' said Amber.

'Because I didn't want to freak you out,' said LB.

'And neither of you tell me this?' said Kelly. 'Before I agree to swap rooms?'

'"Agree to"?' said Amber. She shook her head. 'Unbelievable.'

'What?' said Kelly.

Amber looked around at the others. 'OK . . . not to add to the freakery. But . . . I think . . . I *saw* something too. On the corridor on the first night. This kind of black shadow.'

'That you could make out in the blackness,' said Kelly.

'Exactly,' said Amber. 'That was the weird part. But there was a kind of bluey glow.'

'Where down the corridor?' said Kelly.

'Where it divides off – girls left, boys right. But going straight ahead.'

'What's down there?' said Kelly.

Amber shrugged. 'I don't know. I presume there are some kind of rooms, but you've seen it – it's a dead end, and it's blocked off with those wooden things, like when windows are boarded up.'

'And do you think,' said Kelly, leaning in. 'It was . . . a ghost?'

Amber, fear flickering in her eyes, looked at Rupert. 'No, I don't,' she said, without looking Kelly's way.

90

'But seriously, we could literally be sleeping in what used to be wards,' said Kelly. 'Or electric shock rooms or—' She shrugged.

'A nice pastel-coloured day room,' said Rupert, patting Amber's hand. 'I'd say the school was definitely some kind of outbuilding,' said Lockie.

'Slaughterhouse,' said Kelly.

'Morgue,' said LB.

'I can't believe that Johnny didn't let your dad know in advance,' said Amber.

'What difference would it have made?' said LB. 'And he probably did know. He knew I'd love it.'

'We need to *know*,' said Rupert, leaning in, voice low, 'what we are sleeping in, eating in, learning in . . .'

'Why?' said Kelly.

'Oh my God – for regaling people with stories!' said Rupert. '"Did you know I once read Gaelic in an Irish madhouse?"'

'Zero plans to stay friends with Irish people,' said Amber.

'Let's just ask Johnny,' said Kelly. 'He's probably got a map—'

'Building plan,' said Lockie. 'And site plan.'

'Thank you, Lockie's dad,' said Kelly.

Lockie shrugged. 'They're all over his office.' He held

his hands out wide to indicate size.

'Would Johnny have them, though?' said Rupert. 'And would he just hand them over to us?'

Lockie shook his head. 'There's no way Johnny would encourage us – he's keeping the asylum thing on the down low for when the hotel happens.'

Rupert nodded. 'Guests would be calling to make sure they weren't staying in creepy places. "I'll stay in *this* room!" – some staff dining room the loons were barred from – "But I won't stay in *that* room!" – the brow bar for the criminally insane, where they file down their actual brow bone.'

Kelly straightened in her seat. She gasped. 'Plans! Oh. My. God.' She smiled at everyone. 'You know, it pays to complain to the management.'

'Do *not* complain to him about this,' said LB.

'No,' said Kelly. 'No need. I just . . . or one of us just needs to get into his office. Because when I was in there for *my* complaining and *his* unboxing of the hoodies, there was this folder marked Plans –' she held her hands as wide as Lockie had – 'beside some hardback books with those building drawings and design stuff and I remember thinking, why couldn't he just write his plans down in a notebook like a normal person?'

'Well, Detective Warner,' said Rupert, 'the secret is

out: Johnny Owner has big plans for the place.'

Everyone started to laugh until Amber eyeballed everyone into silence and said, '*Cuinteoir!*' through gritted teeth, just as Réiltín arrived at the table.

'*Dia dhuit, Réiltín,*' said Rupert. *Hello, Réiltín.*

Kelly shot him a look he ignored.

'*Dia is muire dhuit,*' said Réiltín. She looked at Kelly and tilted her head to take her away from the table.

Kelly mouthed at Rupert, '*What the . . . ?*' but she got up and went over to Réiltín.

'*No one is allowed to move rooms any more,*' said Réiltín in Irish.

'We've done our room move,' said Kelly. 'Where else am I going to go? The padded cells? With you?'

She spun around, walked back to the table and sat down. She glanced over to where Réiltín was walking away, ponytail swinging.

She's not supposed to have an ass like that.

Johnny was driving down the drive past the college when he saw Réiltín sitting cross-legged on the grass, studying her clipboard. He beeped the horn and waved. She came over to him.

'How are you getting on?' said Johnny.

Réiltín smiled. 'Great. Thank you.'

Johnny laughed. 'Well, well done. You're a trooper. And I like to reward troopers. So, two things – or should I say two surprises? OK – I'll tell you the first one: I want to pay you for these three weeks.'

Réiltín frowned. 'Really?'

'Well,' said Johnny 'I know you're a volunteer. But would you have actually volunteered for this?'

Réiltín laughed. 'Maybe not. Thank you.'

'Wait till you see your next surprise,' said Johnny. 'I'm heading to Galway to collect it now.' He beeped and drove off.

Réiltín walked away, happy and bemused. She laughed a little laugh – Kelly Warner was, basically, responsible for providing her an income. A sense of unease quickly settled over her, as it always did when it came to Kelly. Because, realistically, what Johnny was paying her was danger money.

At dinner that night, Rupert opened his notebook to a clean double-page spread, and titled it: Operation HOP.

'Operation Hands On the Plans,' said Rupert. 'Also: hop in and hop out before you get caught. For this, I nominate LB.'

'What?' said LB.

'Everyone else would have to break in,' said Rupert.

'And even though I've no doubt Kelly would happily do that, we don't want her to be kicked out just yet. You, however, LB, and sorry to use your celebrity status—'

LB narrowed her eyes. 'By association.'

'The *plan* I recommend,' said Rupert, 'is a very simple one, like all good plans. You ask Johnny to use the phone. You say you need to call your dad urgently – make sure you refer to him as "Antsy" though as a reminder of his fame – and you pick some issue that no normal person would have, to create confusion and, therefore, have permission granted, because Johnny won't want to admit to not understanding rock star terminology slash problems.'

LB didn't blink. Until Rupert waved his hand in front of her face.

'If it makes it easier,' said Rupert, 'focus on the parts that are the truth and not a crime. You want to call your dad. That is the truth. Just don't focus on the fact that it's a truth that you're using as a distraction to facilitate you committing a crime.'

'Stop!' said LB. 'I'm freaking out. 'So, do I actually call home?'

'She said "Yes"!' said Rupert. 'And yes – why not call your dad? He's probably a little deaf from all the drums, so he won't hear the rustle of paper as you rifle through private documents and steal one.'

95

'Oh my God,' said LB, 'why am I doing this?'

'Just go for it,' said Kelly. 'Just be a celebrity offspring for once in your life.'

'You're doing it for us,' said Rupert. 'The truth is, it's the only entertainment we have.'

'And what if my dad doesn't answer the phone?' said LB.

'Phone a friend,' said Kelly. 'Just not us, obvs.'

Rupert stood in the hallway off the lobby for moral support. The others gathered in Amber's room. Half an hour later, LB and Rupert came bounding up the stairs to them.

'Oh my God,' said LB, eyes bright, bending forward and pulling a rolled-up sheet of paper out from under her hoodie. 'I can't believe I did that!'

'This is her villain origin story,' said Rupert. 'Remember this.'

'Johnny was gone, though,' said LB. 'So it was just Réiltín. There wasn't a problem.'

'Did you talk to your dad?' said Kelly.

'Voicemail,' said LB. 'So I pretend-talked to him. I just kept saying, "I can't hear you over the music." What could Réiltín do?'

They spread the architectural drawing out on the bed, weighing it down with four of Amber's crystals.

'So this is the original plan of the asylum,' said Rupert.

'I literally never understand these drawings,' said Kelly.

'Wow,' said Amber. 'It's shaped like . . .'

'Like a dumb-bell,' said Kelly.

'So there are matching buildings at each end,' said Amber. 'One is the administrative block, where we are, and the other is the . . .' She squinted. *Admissions,*' she read. 'For the actual asylum. *Doctors' Rooms.* Stuff like that.'

'Basically,' said Rupert, 'the architects did a copy-and-paste, before it was even invented. Lodge at one end – "That drawing turned out well – same again!" West end!'

Amber drew her finger along the corridor where their rooms were. '*Offices.*'

Rupert smiled and put a reassuring hand on her shoulder. 'No ghost is ever going to haunt an administrative building.'

Lockie reached over to the drawing, gently slid the crystals off it, and rotated it 180 degrees.

'We're in the asylum, lads.' He pointed to their corridor. 'And we're sleeping in the wards.'

15

Rupert arrived downstairs for breakfast at six thirty, with two books under his arm. He had always loved the out-of-hours stillness in places designed to be filled with life – before most people were up, or after they had gone to bed. In their haunted wards. Amber's attic, it transpired, was the only bedroom that had been created from thin air. Amber was good with energy. Meaning no one wanted to know what the classrooms used to be. No one was to be encouraged to steal those plans. Rupert found a quiet place to sit, and took a calm look around what he knew was the dining room of the asylum doctors, before reaching for his books. One was an Irish book and, inside that, the one he really wanted to read – a book of poetry in his comfort language – English. His books of ghost stories were now packed.

He opened his Irish book with the enthusiasm of

someone who forgot it was hiding something, then gasped and quickly picked it up and started to read. After a few minutes, he heard the sound of plates being slid off plates, cutlery clanging, cups hitting saucers. He looked up and caught a side view of a waiter, sleeves rolled up to his elbows, leaning over a trolley, caught in a wide shaft of morning sunlight.

Flaxen-Haired Country Boy in Breakfast Servitude.

Rupert returned to his book, then glanced up again at the precise time the waiter was facing him, an oversized salt grinder in one hand, pepper pot in the other. Rupert's heart skipped, terrifying him. He wanted to speak, but his brain had slid onto the floor like the poetry. The two of them were now in an awkward eye lock.

'*Freastalaí!*' Rupert blurted, eyes bright with pride that he knew the Irish word for 'waiter'.

'*Dalta!*' said the waiter, who knew all the Irish words. And definitely the one for 'student'.

Rupert wanted to apologise for the dramatic labelling, but had none of the vocabulary. Instead, he asked him his name.

'Tadhg,' said the waiter.

'Rupert.' *And yes, I do take Tadhg to be my lawful wedded husband.*

A sudden movement at the door drew their attention.

It was Kelly's head – dark hair, glossy and straight, make-up dewy – making a tentative scan of the room before committing. When she saw Rupert, her body followed, and when she saw Tadhg, it moved with more deliberation. Tadhg's gaze followed her from entrance to arrival at Rupert's side. She flopped down in front of Rupert, her eyes sparkling, her smile as wide as the one she had swept from his face with a flick of her hair and hips.

Burnt-Sienna-Haired Student in Breakfast Heartbreak.

Réiltín checked her watch as she rushed down the hallway – seven thirty a.m. Johnny had called her into his office as soon as she arrived in the lobby and sent her immediately down to the kitchen. She walked in and screamed. It was her very best friend in the world.

'Tadhg!'

'Rézer!' he said, throwing his arms around her.

'Why aren't you in Dublin?' said Réiltín.

'Because Johnny made me an offer I couldn't refuse!' said Tadhg. 'Paying both of us! Twice what I was getting in Dublin!'

Johnny walked in and smiled at Réiltín. 'Surprise!'

Rupert sat in class looking over at Kelly, the beautiful thief. But Tadhg could not possibly be her type. But then, could Kelly go anywhere without locking on to the closest available guy? *Oh my God. I locked onto the closest available guy too. Oh no – is Kelly my role model? Am I the gay Kelly? Do I even know how to be gay? What would I even do with Tadhg? If he proposed, obviously I'd say yes. But the grey areas. He's probably straight. But what was Our First Stare about? Why was that awkward? Oh my God. It was me. Acting alone. A threat. And he was just reacting like when you see a bear and you're not supposed to move. But he did move his eyeballs. Onto Kelly. Which was a normal reaction to Kelly. Nine times out of ten, she was the best-looking girl in the room – the kind that makes girlfriends tighten their grip on their boyfriend's hand. Or boyfriend tighten his grip on imaginary boyfriend's hand. While walking on the beach.*

Rupert and Tadhg, Shoreline, Sunset, Galway.

No – *Rupert and Tadhg, Dusk . . .*

No – *Tadhg and—*

'Rupert! said Miss Breathnach. And he jumped and everyone laughed, and he understood that this was 'the third time!' she had called him – and the cloud-shaped heart dispersed.

That night, Kelly woke up again, heart pounding, aware of sobbing, not sure if it was from her own throat or a sound from her nightmare. It was neither, she realised, when a desperate wailing rose from the silence, seeming to hum from the four walls. She froze. It stopped. Then started again. *Seriously. Here too?* And she wasn't even in the creepy attic. She turned to LB, who was fast asleep, her peaceful doll face momentarily soothing. The moaning stopped. But just long enough for Kelly to let out a breath. This time the silence was broken with choking sobs. Kelly curled into a ball. She didn't want to wake LB. Kelly twisted onto her side, at least where one ear was closed off by the pillow. But she could still hear the moans and, muffled, they were almost creepier.

16

The following evening, Lockie arrived late for dinner. Everyone looked up when he walked in.

'Aw, Locks,' said Amber, 'I'm so sorry about Clare.'

He sat down. Amber squeezed his hand. 'Her dad will calm down.'

'I don't think so,' said Lockie.

'Well, maybe it wasn't meant to be, then,' said Kelly. 'What? Am I not allowed an opinion here?'

'Her father is a fool!' said Rupert. 'But next time, would you please tell me, so you are not suffering in silence?'

'There is no silence, Rupe, sharing a room with you,' said Lockie.

Rupert gasped. Everyone laughed.

'And that's why I love it,' said Lockie.

Kelly sat back and clapped her hands. 'So, what are we doing tonight?'

They all looked at her.

'What?' said Kelly.

'Homework?' said LB.

'Are you serious?' said Kelly.

'Have you seen what we got?' said LB. 'That's like two hours' work. Minimum.'

Kelly shook her head. 'Unreal. Can I copy yours?'

'Of course,' said LB.

'Is it going to be like this every night?' said Kelly.

'Amber's offered to do oracle card readings tomorrow night,' said LB.

'*Oh, well then,*' Kelly mouthed to LB, with an eye roll. She turned to the others. 'So, card readings after our one phone call home from prison in Johnny's office, with Réiltín earwigging.'

'Is anyone going to check what number we actually call?' said Lockie.

'Don't do it,' said Rupert.

Lockie sighed.

'Do you have the Rock Paper Scissors deck I got you?' said Kelly to Amber. 'Where were we again, when I gave it to you? It's such a cool deck. Oh my God – camping! Do you remember? Nightmare. Mom got me all the stuff and literally all of it is stuffed into a rucksack in the attic.'

'Aw, I don't have that one with me,' said Amber.

Kelly lowered her head onto the table. 'Homework in summer.'

'My advice,' said Rupert, standing up, 'is you'll enjoy these three weeks—'

Kelly's head snapped back up. 'Literally, no.'

'I'm just saying,' said Rupert, 'if you come to terms with the reality now—'

'No!' said Kelly.

'Then you wouldn't have to fight against it so hard,' Rupert finished.

'I'm not fighting against it,' said Kelly, pushing herself up from the table. 'I just think you're all boring bitches.'

She paused, then walked away, leaving a layer of mood behind her that settled over the group.

That night, Réiltín stood at the sink in her bathroom, rubbing moisturiser into her face. She paused. She heard what she thought was a knock on the door, but it was so gentle she didn't rush to open it. It came again. She walked out into the bedroom and this time, when she heard it again, she went to the door. She opened it a crack. It was Marcus Loughnane, eyes red-rimmed and puffy.

'Is everything OK?' said Réiltín, completely forgetting to use Irish.

Lockie nodded. 'Just . . . I need to ask you something

105

and . . . just . . . will you promise not to tell anyone?'

Réiltín nodded. 'Sure.' Then: 'I mean, obviously, that depends on what it is.'

'OK.' He paused. 'Can I come in?'

Réiltín hesitated, then opened the door wide. Lockie ducked in.

'Um . . . do you want to sit down?' She gestured around the room randomly, but really there was only the bed and the dressing-table stool to sit on. The chair at her desk was stacked with books. Her desk was stacked with more.

Lockie was momentarily distracted. 'Wow. The books. Will you read all of them?'

Réiltín blushed. 'Probably.'

'In three weeks?' said Lockie.

'Probably. Plus, I've got . . .' She trailed off, suddenly doubting that Marcus Loughnane would care about anything personal.

'If I ask you something,' said Lockie, 'like, as the boss here—'

'Uber boss,' said Réiltín.

Lockie gave a surprised laugh.

Silence descended. Lockie stared at the ground.

'Is there something you need?' said Réiltín.

Lockie looked up at her, eyes nervous. He took a deep breath. 'Look, I know we're not supposed to have phones.

106

That's fine, I get it. And no Wi-Fi. But . . .' He glanced over at her laptop. 'Do you have internet?'

'Yes,' said Réiltín. 'Sorry.'

'Yeah, but you're working,' said Lockie.

Réiltín looked at him. 'I can't give you the code if that's what you're about to ask. Johnny would kill me.'

'What if I just used it once?' said Lockie. 'And you can change it afterwards, and I won't tell anyone you gave it to me—'

Réiltín shook her head. 'I can't.'

Lockie paused, then looked her directly in the eye. 'OK. Look – if I tell you why . . . I hope you can help.'

He walked over to the bed, sat down, and broke down in tears.

Amber sat on her bed, doing a reading for herself from the La Luna oracle deck. One card flew out and landed on the floor in front of the window.

She picked it up. It said HOWL and underneath was an illustration of a wolf howling at the moon. At the bottom was the line *Set your Pain Free*. Amber felt a shift in her stomach. She'd set her pain free before. It was the colour of blood. And she'd set it free with scissors. But it didn't howl. It was the quietest pain she had ever felt.

17

Réiltín woke up the next morning and her first thoughts were: *I have never been in a bedroom with a guy in my entire life. Ever. Not even Tadhg. And I go straight to Marcus Loughnane. Having a breakdown.*

Kelly sat on the picnic bench outside the college, her feet up beside Lockie.

'Rub my ankles – they're freezing,' said Kelly.

'I'm too hungry,' said Lockie.

'Stop,' said Kelly. 'It wasn't my fault.'

'So,' said Rupert, 'when you said at breakfast, "Guys, I'm ready to go – you go get your stuff; I'll sort lunches," and then you didn't, the fault is—'

'I was talking to Tadhg!' said Kelly.

Rupert massaged the stabbing sensation in his chest.

'Talking to him while nowhere near the counter

where he works,' said Amber.

'I was distracted, and then I had to go,' said Kelly.

'The End,' said Rupert.

Beside him, Amber glanced up sharply. 'Did you realise that our last night here falls on the night of the full moon?'

Kelly delivered the same line in a witchy voice.

Amber smiled. 'So . . . I kind of had this idea. 'The full moon, obviously, has always been associated with lunacy. And I was thinking what better place—'

'Not the "what better place" thing again,' said Rupert. 'It never ends well.'

'To perform a full-moon ritual,' Amber continued, 'than on top of Carraig na nGealt?'

'Literally name any other place,' said Rupert. 'All the places except that.'

'Why not?' said Amber.

'Ghost-loons,' said Rupert.

'You love ghosts!' said Amber and LB.

'I said ghost-*loons*,' said Rupert. 'Who probably only come out under a full moon.'

'Would you seriously be freaked out going over there?'

'I was joking about the ghosts,' said Rupert. 'I told you already – it's the "chiselled" steps! Which you know are not going to be smooth and evenly spaced. I will also be terrified by the height, the climb, the sea . . .'

'Come on!' said Amber. 'There is nowhere else we could be closer to the moon, on a site known for its healing properties, and—'

'Lunatics!' said Rupert.

'Why do we need "healing"?' said Kelly. 'There's nothing wrong with us.'

'Can I just find out first what a full-moon ritual actually is?' said Lockie.

'Does it involve him taking off his pants, he wants to know,' said Kelly.

'The full moon is about things being illuminated,' said Amber, 'things being brought to the light so you can deal with them—'

Lockie sucked in a breath. 'Don't know if I like that idea.'

'Ooh,' said Kelly, 'what's Lockie got stashed in the dark?' She turned to Amber. 'Things like what?'

'I don't know,' said Amber. She let out a breath, gathered her thoughts. 'It's about letting go of things, or people, or behaviours, or beliefs, or . . . or whatever. And you release them. Like, "I release being judgemental." Or "I let go of beating myself up," or "I release negative thinking." Whatever.' She shrugged. 'You have a think about it, and you write down your list and give them all to me. And then, on the night, we light a little fire and burn them.'

'Do we have to read them out?' said LB.

'No,' said Amber. 'And I don't read them either. Unless you want me to.'

Kelly looked confused.

'OK,' said Amber, 'say there's something in your life that's not working for you, like . . . like you always run away from conflict. The full moon will bring you a conflict that you can't run away from, so you have to face it.'

'So basically we're all going to be up there having fights,' said Kelly.

Rupert shook his head. 'She said, "people who *run away from conflict*". Not people who run towards it, like those missing pets' reunions with their owners.'

'Or Lockie running into the arms of whoever his next girlfriend—'

Lockie sprung up from the table. 'Screw you, Kelly.'

As he strode away, he side-stepped a guy with a boxy freezer bag coming towards them. He slung the bag onto their table.

'I believe you went off without your lunch,' said Tadhg, unzipping the bag. He took out sandwiches neatly wrapped in greaseproof paper, and handed them around. Then he handed around drinks. Everyone perked up.

'That's the sweetest thing ever, thank you,' said LB.

'No bother,' said Tadhg.

Rupert watched him, speechless. *What a beautiful person . . . who has clearly taken a shine to Kelly, otherwise why would he be saving her right now?*

'This is for you,' Tadhg was saying.

LB slapped Rupert's arm to focus him. Rupert looked up. Tadhg was smiling at him, handing him his sandwich and a can of Coke. Rupert's heartbeat quickened as he took them from him.

'*Cineáltas,*' said Rupert. *Kindness.*

Tadhg laughed, then nodded, and walked away. Rupert watched him until he disappeared into the crowd. He looked down at his sandwich. In block capitals at the centre, Tadhg had written CEAPAIRE! *Sandwich.* Rupert laughed a little hysterically, but nobody noticed. They were all too busy eating.

Student Savages On Bench. Galway.

In one sense, an everyday scene. In another, a charming courtship story for a wedding speech.

18

Friday night, after dinner, Lockie went straight to Johnny's office to call his dad. When his father picked up, Lockie could hardly hear him over the background noise.

'Dad?' said Lockie. 'Dad?'

'Hello? Hello . . . who's this?'

Lockie scowled at the phone. 'Dad? It's Lockie. Where are you?'

'I'm out!' said his Dad. 'In a bar!'

Lockie could hear a booming male voice in the background, and a great blast of a laugh. 'Sorry, son—'

'Having a good night? Out with the lads?' Lockie was gripping the edge of the desk, his knuckles white. For a moment, the only sound at the other end of the phone was happy drinkers, clinking glasses and faint music.

'How's college?' said his dad. 'Are you getting on all right?'

'I'm having a brilliant time,' said Lockie. 'A brilliant *day*.'

'Listen, you know . . .' His dad trailed off. There was another explosion of laughter from the bar. 'By the way,' said his dad, raising his voice over it, 'did you make a charge on my credit card last night?'

'How did you even see that already?' said Lockie.

'Ha!' said his dad. 'I get notified now. Were you hoping to get away with it? What did I get for my ninety euros? I thought you weren't meant to be near the internet. The whole point—'

'You got ninety euros of someone trying to fix my head,' said Lockie.

There was a silence. 'What?' his dad said. 'I can't hear you—'

'Did you not remember the name?' said Lockie. 'It's my old counsellor. We had a Zoom session.'

'Right, right . . . Listen . . . don't worry about the money . . .'

'I won't.'

'And I was going to say to you, just . . . I know this is a hard day for you. For both of us.'

Lockie shook his head. '*Unbelievable*,' he mouthed. 'Yeah, Dad. It is.'

'Is this the first year we weren't together?'

'Yup.'

'Well, look . . . don't put yourself under too much pressure down there. I wouldn't have offered you a grand for every H in the Leaving if I thought I was going to have to hand it over.' He laughed.

Lockie didn't.

'Come on – you're about as academic as your old man and I'm not doing too badly, am I?'

'Dad?' said Lockie, lowering the phone. 'Dad? I can't hear you. Dad . . .'

Réiltín sat at the front desk, fingertips paused over her keyboard, eyes down, body braced. The office door was yanked open and Lockie strode through. He paused and spoke in Irish: '*I'm sorry. For the noise.*'

'*Don't worry about it,*' she replied, also in Irish. She paused. '*I hope you're OK.*'

Lockie stopped abruptly in front of her and continued in broken Irish. '*How are you so good at everything?*'

Réiltín's eyes widened. 'We can speak in English if you like. As long as you don't tell Johnny.'

Lockie smiled.

'And I'm not good at everything,' said Réiltín.

'But . . . your Irish is amazing. How do you remember everything?'

115

'I . . . I like learning,' said Réiltín, making a *Yikes!* face. 'But also, I have tricks.'

Lockie nodded. 'Tricks?'

'Yes,' said Réiltín. 'Different types, depending. And I use the memory palace thing.'

'I've heard of it,' said Lockie, 'but I haven't a clue.'

'Basically, you match objects in a room to things you want to remember. It has to be a room you're really familiar with. And also you attach a visual to it too that's really crazy because then it's easier to remember. So . . .' she looked around. 'That yellow vase is right inside the front door, so it's object number one. And if I wanted to remember your name, I'd picture something crazy, like you holding that yellow vase over your head then smashing it onto the ground like the Hulk, and you're wearing a lock around your neck so I remember Lockie.'

Lockie nodded. 'I like that.'

'It really works. Memory champions use it.'

The double doors swung open as Kelly pushed through from the hallway with both hands. Her stride faltered when she saw Lockie leaning on the front desk and Réiltín smiling up at him.

Kelly raised an imaginary phone to her ear.

Réiltín gestured towards the office. Kelly walked around her into the office, making a face at Lockie as she passed. He ignored her.

'We speak in mime,' said Réiltín.

'I might try that myself,' said Lockie, looking away.

Réiltín's eyes widened.

Rupert was next to bounce through the door, just as Kelly appeared from behind the office door, pointedly ignoring Réiltín and Lockie. To Rupert, she made a phone call gesture with her hand, followed by a thumbs down.

'Ooh,' said Rupert, looking at Réiltín and speaking in Irish. *'Can I have the minutes she didn't use?'*

'What do you mean, minutes?' said Kelly. 'It's a normal phone.'

'I know, but we're still timed,' said Rupert. 'It costs money.'

'Who are *you* calling?' said Kelly, eyes narrowed.

'My dad!' said Rupert. 'Who else?'

'You're such a weirdo,' said Kelly. 'What would you talk to your dad about for half an hour?'

'Oh my God!' said Rupert, throwing his arms up. 'Where do I even start?'

'I'd say the longest I've ever been on the phone to my mom is six minutes.'

'I love my dad!' said Rupert. 'What's wrong with that?'

'Not a thing,' said Lockie, pushing himself up off the

desk. He put a hand on Rupert's shoulder, and squeezed. 'Not a thing.'

He started to walk away, then paused. 'It's my mom's anniversary today. And I'm down here. And my dad's out getting drunk with his mates.'

19

Amber sat on her bed, her oracle decks spread out in a row. There was incense burning, tea lights flickering on the bedside cabinets, crystals in little groups, and more lined up on the narrow windowsill.

Rupert arrived on the top step. 'What in the Attic Atmos Success Story is this?' He sat down on the bed. 'Now, so we're clear. Whatever cards come out here, we'll be interpreting them as "Eternal love: Tadhg".'

'What?' said Amber.

'Yes,' said Rupert. 'Hear how gravely I said that. I'm terrified.' He looked at the desks. 'You're not using any sinister decks, are you?'

'I told you – I've only ever had one of those. So nothing sinister here.'

'Did you know it was Lockie's mum's anniversary today, by the way?'

'No,' said Amber. 'Poor Lockie.'

Rupert nodded. 'And his dad was just out with the lads when he rang.' He shook his head.

'Imagine your dad doing that,' said Amber.

'No,' said Rupert. 'Even . . . all this time later.'

Amber patted his hand. 'All this time' would always be whatever age Rupert was.

The door at the bottom of the stairs opened, and Kelly walked up, batting the light cord out of her way. She looked around. 'Love this vibe,' she said. 'I was like Worst Tenant Ever . . . Ooh – pretty sky,' she said, bending down to pick up one of the oracle decks from the bed. '"Starscape Oracle",' she read. '"The stars know more than you." Definitely when it comes to Irish. Probably when it comes to most things.' She opened the box, pulled out the cards, and started looking through them. She stopped abruptly, and turned to Amber. 'I forgot! I'm not supposed to touch them, am I? Why do I always do that?'

'Don't worry about it,' said Amber. 'I'll do my thing. Think of your question.'

Kelly closed her eyes. 'OK . . . got it.'

As Amber shuffled, three cards flew out of the deck – two landed face down on the bed, one face up on the floor. Amber slid the cards towards her, then bent down and picked up the one that was on the floor.

'OK,' said Amber. 'You got "Shine, Baby"—'

'As always,' said Kelly.

'"One is All" and "See by my Light",' said Amber. She handed Kelly the booklet to cross-reference the cards.

'*You* read them for me!' said Kelly. 'I love it when you read them.'

'I know,' said Amber, 'but I won't have enough time.'

'Plus,' said Rupert, 'you skipped the queue.'

'I thought you were finished!' said Kelly. 'You were just sitting there.'

'Yes,' said Rupert, 'clearly with no sense of what my future held, if you bothered to look close enough.'

Amber closed her eyes. 'I'm sensing . . . eternal love?'

Amber and Rupert laughed.

Kelly's attention was on the booklet. 'I like these messages.' She nodded. 'The stars are my friends.' She paused. 'Except Twinkle, twinkle, little—'

'Hello?' The voice came from downstairs.

'*Réiltín!*' mouthed Rupert.

Amber closed her eyes. 'Yes?'

'It's Réiltín. I'll just leave your bedlinen here on the stairs. It's every Friday.' She paused. 'You have to make your own beds.'

Kelly's eyes widened and she collapsed back on the bed and had a silent tantrum.

Rupert took Kelly's hand when Réiltín was gone, and pulled her up into a sitting position.

'Well done,' he said. 'For choosing to avoid that conflict.'

'I choose to avoid loads of conflicts,' said Kelly. 'Stop . . . attacking me.'

'"Attacking,"' said Rupert. 'Me? I'm—'

'A walking missing pets' reunion,' said Kelly.

Rupert frowned. 'You came up with it!' said Kelly. 'When you were attacking me about running towards conflict.'

'First off,' said Rupert, 'I come up with so many things I need my own quotations bible, literally *Rupert's Quotations* by Rupert for Rupert. And stop saying "attacking". I have never attacked anyone in my life. To date. None of us, however, knows the future.' He turned to Amber. 'Let's see what the cards say.'

'Pick your deck, ask your question,' said LB.

Rupert pointed to the Wild Wayfarer oracle deck. 'A tame wayfarer would be no fun,' said Rupert. 'A to B, Stick to the Path, Plod Along.' He paused. 'Oh, my question.' He closed his eyes. 'OK, go.'

Amber shuffled for almost thirty seconds. One card hopped out beside her, face up.

Stick to the Path.

Rupert gasped. 'You have to be kidding me.' He read

the message on the card. '"There are times to be wild, and times to be tame. Firm feet, slow progress wins the game."' He handed it back to Amber. 'I'd like to complain to the management.'

Amber slid it back in, and started shuffling the cards again. 'Kelly, is LB coming?'

Kelly looked up from the open booklet. 'She is – seriously – studying on a Friday night.'

'I think you're going to have to get used to that,' said Rupert.

'Yup,' said Amber.

'We wouldn't all be backstage VIPs,' said Rupert, 'if LB was going to come here and behave like . . . a backstage VIP.'

20

TWO WEEKS LATER – EXAM DAY

Kelly sat in the classroom, scowling out of the window at the blue sky. She was holding her pen between her index fingers, pushing it back and forth. She turned to the empty desk beside her, then checked the clock on the wall above the blackboard. Ten minutes to eight. Where the hell was LB? Her chest tightened at the thought of having to do the exam on her own. She shifted in her seat, checked the door, checked the time. LB was never late for exams. She had been ready when Kelly was leaving. She said she'd be there in five minutes. Kelly looked out of the window again. Then she heard someone flop down on the chair next to her, and she turned to see one of the guys from the céilí.

'Is this yours?' he said, handing Kelly the pencil case she had used to hold LB's place. 'How's it going?' he said.

'Oh my God – get up!' hissed Kelly. 'It's there for a reason. My friend's sitting there.'

'What are you going to do?' he said. 'Throw me across the room?'

'Very funny,' said Kelly. 'But get up.'

He narrowed his eyes. 'Do you mean Antsy's daughter? That friend?'

Kelly's eyes widened. 'How do you know who she is?'

'Eh? You told us, the night of the céilí?'

'No, I didn't.'

'Yes, you did. You told me you'd get my da tickets to one of the gigs.'

Kelly paused. 'I was only joking.'

'Well, it got you a few drinks off us, fair play to you. No hard feelings. We're all afraid of you now anyway.' He laughed. 'Anyway, your friend, Blondie, she bailed on you.'

'Yeah, right,' said Kelly. 'There's no way—'

'Calm down,' he said, 'but I'm not joking you. As of five minutes ago, she was bawling crying and running in the exact opposite direction from this classroom.'

'What?' said Kelly. 'Which opposite? Back to our room?'

'How would I know where your room is?' he said.

'Oh my God – point me in the direction,' said Kelly. 'There's like six minutes to go.' She paused. 'Was she all right?'

'The bawling crying girl? I don't know . . . what do you think?'

Kelly looked out of the window again, then back at him. 'Should I go after her?'

He shrugged. 'I don't know. I mean . . . how good a friend are you?'

21

PRESENT

Everyone was sitting at dinner when Kelly walked in, arms raised.

'Céilí, Sunday night, bitchanna! We're going off site! They give us zero entertainment until five days before the exam, which I'm loving. If I get drunk enough, I can sleep right through it. The exam, obviously.' She paused. 'My thinking is, to liven things up, we get lovely Tadhg to get us some alcohol.'

Amber looked at her. 'Réiltín's bestie? Good luck with that.'

'I actually don't think Réiltín's *told* him about—'

'*Your* bullying?' said Rupert.

'Bullying?' said Kelly. 'Our "differences" I was going to say.'

'Why would you think he hadn't told her?' said Amber.

'Because,' said Kelly, 'he never gives me dirty looks, like, on her behalf.' She turned to Rupert. 'And he's really nice to you. You're always chatting away to him at breakfast.'

'What's that look?' said Rupert. 'I won't be asking him to get alcohol.'

LB looked up at Kelly. 'Anyway, did you see the bar? Empty of all alcohol.'

'Do you think they emptied it because we were coming?' said Rupert. 'What were they expecting?'

'Kelly,' said Lockie.

'But what they were not expecting,' said Kelly, 'was my determination. Because there may be no alcohol in the bar, but there's no way they'd go to the trouble of removing it from the *premises*. So it's somewhere in the building. And when we find it—'

'Or,' said LB, 'you could figure out a way of buying some.'

'It tastes better stolen,' said Kelly.

That night, Amber fell asleep studying, and drifted awake surrounded by revision notes. She checked the clock: 02:30. She groaned and sat up. She went over to the desk drawer and pulled it open. No food. She paused, briefly, at the top of the stairs, then crept down. She pushed open the door onto the corridor, and walked along it, the sensor lights coming on as she moved. As she came to the corner to turn right, she heard a sound like crying coming from the short corridor to the left – the boarded-up dead end. Her heart started to pound. She saw a dim line of light on the floor, blinked and it was gone. The moaning stopped. She let out a breath, shook out her hands, then instead of taking the right, she took the left. She braced herself for the light to come on. Nothing. She looked up. In the dark, all she could make out was the metal ring. She walked further along, still no light. None of the overhead lights lit up after one, two, three, four doors. The fifth was the last on the right-hand side. She approached it slowly, then stopped when she heard the sound of movement inside, like the slide of a box, and the clinking of glass. She moved closer again, and could see a sign on the door at a crooked angle: Laundry. She looked at the door opposite and it was Room 6.

Suddenly, Johnny's voice boomed from inside Room 5, way too close to the door: 'Right, well that's that sorted!' Amber jumped, froze, then darted away, taking a right down her corridor, bursting through her door and taking the stairs up in huge strides, falling up the last two. She crawled over to the bed and collapsed onto it. She pulled open the middle drawer of her bedside cabinet where they had left the building plan. She drew her finger down the corridor, where there were six rooms . . . And if that was really a laundry room, then it was the biggest she had ever seen.

Kelly was the last to arrive down for breakfast the next morning. She yawned and looked around at everyone.

'Someone get me food.'

'Have this,' said Amber, pushing an untouched Danish towards her.

'Oh, thank God,' said Kelly, tearing at it. 'And thank you.'

'I can also,' said Amber, 'maybe – even though I fear for you – direct you to the alcohol.'

Everyone gathered in Kelly and LB's room.

'I can't believe it's me again,' said LB.

'For the same reason as before,' said Rupert. 'And it's me again too, as director of criminal enterprise. This time, though, all you have to do is check the door handle and confirm whether or not the door is locked. You're going down a dark hallway too, so you don't have to worry about being seen. Plus, if Johnny or Tadhg or Réiltín or whoever comes, one of us will be on either side on distraction duty. Obviously, we can pretend we were casually walking down whichever corridor, because it's not like we can hide with a light on over our heads.

Either way, though, we can still draw his attention, and all *you* have to do is *ruuuun* all the way down the long one or take a left or right – wherever Johnny has not been redirected to.'

Kelly looked at LB. 'Would it help if I came with you?'

'Yes!' said LB.

'Will it, though?' said Rupert.

Kelly narrowed her eyes at him.

'Yes – come, Kel, please,' said LB. 'And that was the last they saw of Kelly,' said Rupert.

LB took the lead down the corridor, Kelly behind her, holding her hand by the fingers. They slowed as they approached the laundry room. LB reached out tentatively and tried the doorknob. It clicked open.

'Push it in!' hissed Kelly. 'Just have a look.'

LB shook her head.

'Just a tiny bit,' whispered Kelly. 'So the lads won't have to waste their time, if there's just laundry in it.'

'It's pitch dark,' said LB.

Behind them came the rattle of a doorknob. They spun around as the door to Room 6 started to open. Kelly, panicked, shoved LB hard through the door, then closed it behind her.

22

As the door to Room 6 was opening, Kelly hopped a few paces to the boarded-up end of the corridor. She slapped a frown on her face and put her hands on the wood panelling, like she was examining it.

Meanwhile, LB staggered to a stop in the centre of the alleged laundry room. Through a gap in the thick curtains came a single dusty shaft of light. LB looked around in the gloom. There was no laundry. No beer crates. No bottles, apart from the water by the bed. It was simply a bedroom. With a bed. And a figure, under a mound of bedcovers, slowly rolling towards her.

LB's heart was pounding. From the corridor, she could hear the boom of Johnny's voice, and Kelly's high-speed distraction chatter. LB's feet were rooted, eyes fixed on the bed as one skinny arm flopped down on top of the covers, then another, and the figure started to sit up. LB ducked down at the end of the bed, hand over her mouth, knees to her chest. She was facing the door, and was about to crawl for it, super-fast, when she heard the sound of someone settling against the headboard, the flick of a wall light.

'I can see you in the mirror.' It was a woman's voice, low and husky. She cleared her throat.

LB turned her head to an enormous mirror leaning against the wall opposite the bed. She could see herself in an embarrassing ball, half lit by the shaft of sunlight, and the woman in a black strappy top, propped up against a pillow, glowing in the lamplight. She was pale and thin, with a mass of tousled black hair, smudges of mascara under her eyes.

'We look like a theatre performance,' said the woman. She gestured for LB to stand up. LB slowly obeyed. The woman squinted at her.

'You, by the looks of you, must be Lotus Blossom Behan.'

LB's eyes widened.

'I'm Suze,' said the woman. 'I'm Johnny's wife. Or Johnny's my husband . . . Is one better than the other?'

'How do you know who I am?' said LB.

'I know you from when you were little,' said Suze. 'Before all this, Johnny and I owned a club in Dublin. Well, bar, nightclub, restaurant.' She raised her fingers in quotes: '"Beloved by the stars". Wild nights, and mellow Sunday brunch with the family. We used to joke we held the stars in our hands. While they exploded.' She laughed. 'Not your dad, obviously. Very well behaved.'

LB waited.

'Sorry,' said Suze, 'what was I saying? Oh yes – you. So, wild nights and brunch on Sunday, with family. Including little ones. Your parents always brought you when your dad was in town.'

'Wow,' said LB. 'I don't remember that.'

'Well,' said Suze, 'do you ever remember a lift with an entire galaxy on the inside, pressing all the buttons? Up and down, up and down.'

LB's eyes lit up. 'The spaceship! Oh my God. I was obsessed!'

Suze nodded. 'And now, here we are.'

'I'm so sorry for just . . . bursting in. We didn't know anyone was . . . we thought the room was—'

'A laundry room?' Suze nodded. 'No . . . but I am trying to clean up . . . my act.' She paused. 'I'm going through some . . . things. It's unfortunate timing you all being here – on the one hand. And on the other, excellent, because, to be honest, we needed the money. And we love your dad. He's always been good to us . . .' She paused. 'We were good to him too, of course.'

'Well, thank you for having us!' said LB. 'We're having a great time. And the food is great and . . .' She trailed off. She noticed the self-help books stacked on one bedside cabinet, the crumpled tissues on the other.

Suze smiled. 'Go on – ask, whatever it is.'

'Just,' said LB, 'Have you – it's none of my business – but ever been . . . crying at night?'

Suze froze. 'Oh! I didn't expect you to ask that. You can hear that?'

LB nodded. 'Sorry.'

Suze closed her eyes, banged the back of her head on the headboard. 'Johnny Metcalfe, I'll kill you.' She looked at LB. 'These walls were meant to be soundproofed. But Johnny obviously . . .' She sighed. 'Obviously, that costs more money.'

'Sorry for asking about the crying,' said LB. 'It's just the others thought . . . well, I thought too . . . it might be . . .' She shrugged. 'A ghost.'

'Maybe let's keep it that way,' said Suze, nodding firmly. 'Now that I know you can hear me I might do my crying somewhere else. In the rain, maybe.' She laughed. 'So . . . I won't tell if you won't.'

'Not even Johnny?' said LB.

Suze shook her head. 'Not even Johnny.'

'Does Réiltín know you're here?'

Suze nodded. 'But . . . let's neither of us mention our little encounter to her, either.'

LB followed Suze's gaze around the untidy room, the scattered magazines, overfilled boxes, piles of shoes, elegant clothes draped across different surfaces or discarded on the floor.

Suze smiled. 'Not really living my best life, am I?'

Lockie, Rupert and Amber were sitting on Kelly's bed, watching her pace.

'Where is she?' said Kelly. 'Oh my God.'

'Calm down,' said Lockie. 'Seriously, what could have happened to her?'

'But why wasn't she back?' said Kelly. 'Right after she heard me and Johnny leave?'

'We'll ask her on her return,' said Rupert.

'Imagine,' said Kelly, 'trying to come up with a story about why someone like me is standing in the dark, feeling up some random wood?'

'What did you say?' said Lockie.

'Ugh,' said Kelly. 'That's the whole point. I *couldn't* come up with a story. So I pretended I was sleep walking.'

'At eight o'clock.' said Rupert.

'Study nap,' said Kelly.

Rupert and Lockie laughed.

'Shut up,' said Kelly. 'What if someone kidnapped her? Like, they found out who she is.' She gasped. 'Réiltín! She's a total stalker. You know she's obsessed with Antsy.'

'And she's taking her chance now,' said Rupert. 'Réiltín gets McQuaid fired, the email goes out to parents, and the masterplan begins!'

The door opened gently and LB walked in. She locked eyes with Kelly. 'Don't *ever* do that to me again.'

'I saved you!' said Kelly. 'I pushed you to safety.'

'How did you know it was safe?' said LB.

'Otherwise, both of us would have had to be sleepwalking,' said Kelly. 'What would be the chances of that?'

'Oh my God,' said LB. 'That was your excuse.'

'What took you so long anyhow? What were you doing? Was there alcohol in there? Was I right? Only one night to go for a céilí back-up plan.'

23

The céilí was being hosted by local céilí dancers in a GAA club half an hour away from the college.

'Air, people – Jesus!' said Kelly, swaying in the door, pointing to the little row of barely open windows, where the walls met the ceiling. 'It's roasting.' She looked around. 'Is the whole course here?'

'Pretty much,' said Amber.

Kelly took a drink from a plastic bottle of watery orange liquid.

'Kelly's like, "Thank God for Boys for Kelly,"' said Lockie to Rupert.

'Thank God for their vodka,' said Kelly, taking another drink.

'Off-brand, I'm presuming,' said Rupert. 'Shmodka.'

'Does that mean he's going to be here,' said Lockie, 'cashing in?'

'Ew,' said Kelly.

'Be careful is all I meant,' said Lockie.

'Aw, thanks, Locks.' She smiled up at him. He gave her a small smile back.

'Right,' said Kelly. 'I'm going to tell them to open the doors.' She looked around. 'Where's Réiltín? I'll say it to her! Did you see the state of her standing outside the bus with her clipboard, doing her little ticks, and then again as we're getting off the bus in case one of us could have fallen out of it on the way.'

'Oh, look!' said Rupert. 'A table in the furthest corner!' Everyone followed him.

'I'll go to the bar,' said Amber, letting everyone else sit down.

'Get me more orange,' said Kelly. 'So I can actually drink this.'

An hour later, Lockie walked towards them after a break in the dancing, pulling his damp T-shirt away from his stomach.

'These people are insane,' said Lockie.

'Totally,' said Amber, coming up behind him, gesturing back to the locals, who were sitting down, drinking water and laughing. 'They're, like, ninety and they're not even out of breath.'

Rupert was sitting with LB. 'We've only just started breathing again.'

'Where's Kelly?' said Amber.

'With her supplier,' said Rupert, pointing to an open door at the back.

'Oh God,' said Amber.

'I'll go,' said Lockie. 'I need air.'

He came back in after ten minutes. 'OK – she is seriously drunk.' He turned to LB. 'You need to talk to her. Your man is trying to get her to go back to his place.'

'What?' said LB. 'She's not actually—'

'On any level sober,' said Lockie.

'This is a disaster,' said Amber. 'Do you think we should tell Réiltín?'

'What?' said LB. 'No way.'

'I just mean . . . should we *warn* Réiltín,' said Amber. 'There's no way she wants to take on drunk Kelly.'

'No,' said LB. 'We just need to keep them apart. And get Kelly at least sober enough before we leave that we don't have to carry her.'

Everyone looked at LB, expectantly.

'Fine!' she said.

Kelly was surrounded by a group of guys, all laughing and smoking, when LB walked out.

'Kelly,' said LB from a distance. 'Can I borrow you?'

'Yes!' said Kelly. 'That's LB, everyone! My cool friend!'

LB waved. Kelly bounced up to her, and took her into a huddle.

'So that's the guy,' said Kelly. 'Was Lockie telling you? The tall one. And he'll drop me back in the morning.'

'What?' said LB. 'Do you think Réiltín's going to miss you on the bus? What the hell?'

'Ugh,' said Kelly. 'Screw Réiltín.'

'It would have been whoever!' said LB. 'Even if Réiltín was never here, whoever was doing her job would have been doing this.'

'Ugh,' said Kelly.

'OK, seriously,' said LB. 'Come back inside. You can't—'

'Come over and say hi!' said Kelly. 'Come on.'

'No!' said LB. 'Stop acting like we're on holiday. We're not.'

'Since when do you care about any of this?' said Kelly.

'Oh my God – stop trying to make me feel bad for just wanting to do well!' said LB. 'I actually like the idea of going into sixth year with one subject I don't have to worry about.'

'Stop acting like a boring bitch,' said Kelly.

LB flinched. 'I'm not,' she said. 'I just hate this whole "Oh, we're not supposed to do *this*, so let's do it" thing . . .'

141

'No, you don't. You love it. And Johnny's a total scam artist,' said Kelly. 'Him and his imaginary wife.'

'No, they're not,' said LB. 'They're just people who needed to find a new way of making money.'

'Yeah . . . suckering parents.'

'They're not suckering anyone,' said LB. She tried to hand Kelly a bottle of water.

'Are you joking me?' said Kelly, folding her arms. 'Oh my GOD, this place.'

'Why did you even come here?' said LB.

'To hang out with you!' said Kelly. 'Because it's August! Because that's what we do, every summer. What was I going to do? Stay in Dublin on my own?'

'Yes, if you wanted to!' said LB.

'Did you not want me to come?' said Kelly.

'No! Of course I wanted you to come!'

'You're just not happy I'm here now,' said Kelly.

'No!' said LB. 'I am happy. But you're—'

'You're the one who looks miserable!' said Kelly.

LB walked away.

Kelly's shoulders slumped. 'I'm not going to go anywhere. Not without you.'

LB walked back inside, and passed Amber in the hallway.

'Nightmare,' said LB, shaking her head. 'Nightmare.'

24

LB looked across the room and saw Réiltín sitting on her own, her leg swinging. She walked over to her.

'Mind if I sit down?' said LB. 'And speak in English?'

Réiltín was shaken out of her daze. 'Sure. No problem.'

'This is fun,' said LB, looking around. 'I didn't think it would be.'

'Yeah, it is. I love it,' said Réiltín.

One of the older dancers walked past. 'Réiltín! You haven't been up on the floor once tonight!'

'Do you normally dance?' said LB.

Réiltín nodded.

'Are you just sick of it?' said LB.

'No, just chilling,' said Réiltín. 'But I know that an elderly couple could abduct me at any moment.' She mimed being wrestled away onto the dance floor.

LB laughed.

'They've already taken Rupert,' said Réiltín, nodding to where Rupert was in the thick of the action, knees and head high.

'They won't give him back,' said LB.

Rupert came to the end of the line and broke away, dancing towards Amber, light on his feet. He grabbed her hands to try to pull her up.

'Ooh, no,' said Amber, tilting her head to the right.

Rupert followed her gaze to where Kelly was sitting on a bench inside the door, her legs and arms crossed, glaring at Réiltín and LB.

'Allow me,' said Rupert, gently lowering Amber's hands. He skipped over to Kelly and sat down beside her. 'Can I tell you a story?' he said, crossing his leg towards her, sliding closer.

'Once upon a time,' said Rupert, 'there were people, all of whom had different relationships with each other. And no one died. The End.'

Kelly gave him a squinty smile and got up. 'Yeah, thanks for that, Rupe.' She shook her empty bottle. 'Back soon.'

For the last dance, all the tables were pushed back to the walls, and the largest crowd of the night lined up. LB and Réiltín were pushing their table back to the wall.

'Are we going to dance?' said LB.

Réiltín frowned. 'What about . . . will Kelly not be back?'

LB shook her head. 'She's outside.'

Réiltín shrugged. 'OK.'

They moved towards the dancers lining up, and were immediately swept up by a smiling middle-aged couple. LB and Réiltín burst out laughing. The woman placed them into position, raised their hands and clamped them together. LB and Réiltín exchanged awkward smiles.

Amber arrived at Rupert's side and handed him a bottle of water. She followed his gaze to Kelly, who had just hit the dance floor.

'Whatever music the band is playing,' said Rupert, '*I'm hearing Jaws.*'

They watched as Kelly danced and twirled, her smile so wide and drunken it was extending beyond her face in a blur as she was passed from one dancer to the next, clamping her hands hard onto her partners'. Her balance was so off.

Then, her back to Kelly, moving steadily, rationally, rhythmically, soberly, was Réiltín, who had no idea what was coming her way.

Amber sucked in a breath and held it.

'It's *Riverdance* and the river is made of Réiltín's blood,' said Rupert. He craned his neck, up and down, back and forth, as the lines of dancers criss-crossed. 'I'm trying to work it out . . . will they actually meet?'

The stamping of the dancers' feet was getting louder and louder.

Rupert stood up on the bench behind him and pulled Amber up too. 'I need an aerial shot.'

They watched as Kelly was spun into the arms of a short, wide block of a man.

'Uh-oh,' said Amber, 'he's one of those power dancers. He could fling her—'

They watched. 'Oh . . .' said Rupert. 'No – she's holding her own.' He gasped. 'But now she's a bullet. If she can control the aim, and use his fire power . . .'

'She's headed for Réiltín,' said Amber.

Rupert nodded. '*Annnnd* . . . locked on.'

Réiltín was dancing with an older woman who was expertly spinning her around, and, as she was sent to her next partner – a blocky man with a huge smile – Réiltín caught a flash nearby of long dark hair whipping around, and, as she turned again, her partner was passing her on to— Réiltín's eyes shot wide as she was suddenly holding hands with a flushed, glassy-eyed Kelly. The two of them were spinning in a circle, their hands clutched at the centre, but Kelly was stronger and squeezing Réiltín's hands tighter. Then Kelly was leaning back too far, so Réiltín was leaning back too far, and they were spinning faster and faster, but there was no solid centre any more, and tiny Réiltín felt too light to be a counterweight to a drunk Kelly.

Rupert and Amber gasped as they watched the girls spin faster and faster and looser and looser, and saw how the people around them were forced to make room for them, but not in a give-them-the-floor way, but in a save-yourself way, and Rupert and Amber just about stopped breathing when, in a spectacularly inelegant move, Réiltín was flung across the floor, while Kelly remained upright like an accidental bullfighter.

25

LB was the first of the group to Réiltín's side, beating the rush of concerned adults. Réiltín was rising up from the floor on her elbow, inches from a table leg she could have slammed her face into if she hadn't deployed her arms at the right moment.

'Are you OK?' said LB.

'Not really,' said Réiltín, her hair loose, her head hanging, but she looked up and smiled.

'Oh God,' said LB, recoiling.

'What?' said Réiltín.

'You've got blood,' said LB, indicating it was across her teeth.

Réiltín covered her mouth with her hand and started to get up. 'I'll go to the bathroom,' she mumbled.

'Maybe don't move too much,' said LB. 'Just in case. I can get you some water.' She looked around.

'Oh my God,' said Kelly, finally arriving, leaning awkwardly down to speak into Réiltín's face.

Réiltín leaned away.

'Her mouth is cut,' said LB.

'I am so, so sorry,' said Kelly. 'Let me help you up.'

Réiltín shook her head.

'I really am sorry,' said Kelly. Réiltín nodded.

'I . . .' said Kelly. She looked at LB and shrugged. 'You know I'm freakishly strong.' And she looked down at Réiltín. 'And you're tiny.'

LB pointed to Kelly's mouth and said, 'Mints,' and she pointed under her own eyes to send Kelly to the bathroom to fix her mascara.

LB helped Réiltín to her feet and got her to sit at a table. Someone brought her water, someone else was promising her sweet tea was on its way. Lockie arrived with awkward condolences.

Rupert turned to Amber. 'We could not have stopped this. We could not have charged into the middle of a long line of céilí. No one does that. It's a risk even to walk by. It's like getting caught in machinery – you're pulled in by your jumper or your hair . . .'

Amber nodded bleakly. 'We could not have averted that disaster.'

'All we could do was bear witness,' said Rupert. 'We

can go in with clear consciences.'

Rupert and Amber arrived over to the others, and then Kelly was back, smelling of mint and bathroom air freshener.

Beside them sat Réiltín, her hands around a cup of sweet, milky tea, looking up into the least expected circle of concerned faces she could ever have imagined.

'Ré!' said a voice, and everyone turned to see Tadhg push through the crowd.

'Tadhg!' said Rupert. He exchanged excited glances with Amber.

Tadhg nodded as he crouched down to examine Réiltín for injuries.

'*Doctor* Tadhg,' said Réiltín, in Irish.

'Not yet,' said Tadhg, smiling.

It was the first time Rupert had seen them together, seen how relaxed they were in each other's company and how there was nothing romantic on any level about it, but he knew too how blind he would choose to be even if there was. Rupert was about to wonder what Tadhg's friendship with Réiltín might mean for their future together, but he set it aside for now because: *Doctor*.

Back at the hotel, Kelly was propped up on her bed, wiping off her make-up with cotton wool pads.

'I know the whole thing looks bad,' she said, 'but I did not do that on purpose. I swear to God. Like, that would be so dangerous. She could have whacked her head on something and died.'

'You're really lucky she's all right,' said LB. 'She used to do gymnastics and stuff – that's probably why she knew how to land.'

'Oh, you know everything about her now,' said Kelly. She got up and went into the bathroom. 'You were talking to her for ages,' she called out.

'Not ages,' said LB. She could hear the pedal bin opening, the tap running.

'Tadhg was so cute,' said LB, quickly changing the subject. 'Do you think he's gay? Did you see Rupert?'

Kelly walked out of the bathroom, zoned out, focused on getting into bed. She paused. 'Can you imagine, though? You're dancing like crazy and suddenly you're standing there with your arms wrapped around someone you absolutely hate and you're both like, "What the—?"'

'I know,' said LB.

'So it was like she just . . . slipped through my hands,' said Kelly. 'Not in a slippery way, just . . .'

'You were drunk, and your co-ordination was off,' said LB.

Kelly glared at her. 'As if *you've* never been drunk.'

'I know,' said LB. 'But . . .' She didn't finish the sentence, leaving 'but never *that* drunk' unsaid. Because maybe she would get as drunk as Kelly if she wasn't always so conscious of someone taking a photo and posting it somewhere. When she'd been on holiday in Italy two years earlier, on a beach in the middle of nowhere, she was papped, and didn't even know until the photo was up online and there were all these horrific comments about literally every part of her face and body, and she read the first few, and tried to never let her thoughts go there again. She was really good at that. Hearing something horrible then *Slam*, the gate goes down. And if she did it quick enough, she'd never remember. But she hadn't been quick enough that time, and she'd cried and cried and she didn't know how she would have coped if it hadn't been for Kelly, doing all her Kelly things – making her laugh, bringing her random silly toys, junk food, teddy bears, telling everyone at school she was totally fine with the photos and had laughed it all off. Even though Kelly knew that she hadn't, that she'd gone to her mom's nutritionist and worked out every day for a year straight, until her parents had had a talk with her. Now, she just ran every day, and did whatever other exercise she felt like whenever she felt like it. She was still waiting to love her body, but all the compliments Kelly gave her really made a difference.

LB turned to Kelly and smiled. 'Look, everyone's fine.' She pulled back the covers and got into bed. 'And Réiltín knows it was an accident.'

'Did she say that?' said Kelly.

'No,' said LB, 'but of course she knows that.'

Kelly tried to keep her eyebrows from rising.

Réiltín lay in bed, jaw clamped, eyes fixed on the ceiling, body rigid. Her heart was pounding faster and heavier the more she replayed the events of the night. There was something deeply wrong with Kelly Warner. Her stomach tightened at the thought of ever finding out what that was.

26

Two days after the céilí, Kelly was in Lockie and Rupert's room, sitting on Lockie's desk, her feet up on his empty chair.

'When will Lockie be back?' she said, turning to Rupert. He was sitting at his desk, a magazine open on his lap, his long legs crossed, his loafered feet propped up on the dressing table. He held the magazine up for Kelly. 'Simply: *Galway*.' He flicked through the society pages. 'Happy for Bridie and Nuala – they secured hats for the races. Sad for their gentlemen friends. Not ready to release the brown dress shoe, lads. Maybe after the full moon.'

'Did he say,' said Kelly, 'how long he'd be?'

'A run is a run,' said Rupert. 'But exam tomorrow – that's like match day. Does that mean a longer or shorter run? I just don't know. Possibly shorter. So he can stay up later to squeeze more Irish into him.'

'Why aren't you studying?' said Kelly.

'Why aren't you studying?' said Rupert. 'I'm on literally a five-minute break. Round two will be carried out with Amber in the attic for the night.'

'LB refuses to study with me,' said Kelly.

'Would that be because you refuse to study, so it's like an infinity loop?' said Rupert. He turned his attention back to the magazine.

'She's probably going to study with Réiltín,' said Kelly.

Rupert kept turning the pages.

'Her new bestie,' Kelly added.

'Not engaging,' said Rupert. 'Refusing to.'

'I think LB thinks she's her friend,' said Kelly.

'Who thinks the what now?' said Rupert, looking up, eyebrow arched.

'LB thinks Réiltín's her friend, but she's not; she's just a total stalker.'

Rupert frowned.

'Of Antsy!' said Kelly. 'I heard she's got some massive limited-edition signed album art hanging in her bedroom. Like, who buys those except stalkers?'

'Regular fans? With money?'

'Then she's suddenly getting all cosy with Antsy's daughter?' said Kelly.

Rupert gasped. 'It all goes back to McQuaid. She

eliminates the Irish teacher so she can lure LB and all her friends to an isolated Irish college where she speaks in tongues . . . that those friends then pay to learn how to speak in.' He gasped again. 'The cruel possible irony. In fairness, if anyone could organise an elaborate masterplan to . . . what, get her hands on a new poster? . . . it's Réiltín.'

'I'm telling you,' said Kelly, 'she's a stalker. She wants Electric Picnic tickets. She's after a backstage pass for a headliner. I'm telling you. I bet you.'

'Headliner?' Rupert looked up.

'OK – no one's supposed to know that,' said Kelly, eyes wide. 'It's . . . like not even . . . "rumoured". Don't tell LB. She'll kill me.'

'Of course I won't,' said Rupert. He looked up. 'But you do know that means that no – Réiltín is not after tickets to a gig she doesn't know exists.'

'That's why the tickets would be so hard to get!' said Kelly. 'Unless you knew someone!'

Rupert was turning the pages of the magazine steadily, and too fast to be reading it. 'She's actually nice,' he added quietly.

'What?' said Kelly.

'Pardon,' said Rupert.

'Did you say she was nice?' said Kelly.

'I did,' said Rupert.

'You're just saying that,' said Kelly.

'Why would I need to say that?' said Rupert, glancing up.

'Because she's friends with Tadhg.'

'Jealousy,' said Rupert, eyes on the magazine, 'is an ugly undergarment.' He paused, mid-flick of a page. 'Because it's never the outer layer, is it?' He looked up. 'It's always next to the skin.'

LB was sitting at her desk studying, her head in her hand, scanning pages of neatly written Irish vocabulary, some words highlighted in pink with little asterisks beside them.

The door was flung open and Kelly burst in. 'Hello, bitchíocht.'

'Hey,' said LB. 'How were Rupert and Lockie?'

'Lockie is out for a run. And Rupert and Amber are about to join forces in the attic. I, on the other hand, am going for a shower.'

'Are you going to . . .' LB trailed off.

'Who knows?' said Kelly. 'Who knows?'

When she was gone, LB looked over at Kelly's desk, which looked like a cosmetics counter, and at her bed, which was covered in study notes that looked fresh from the printer. She reminded herself this was not her responsibility, and turned back to her revision.

Five minutes later, Kelly came out of the bathroom in a cloud of steam, wrapping her hair up in a turban. 'It is so weird being in the shower in silence,' she said. 'Silent showers are creepy.' She paused at LB's desk. 'How's it going?'

'Good,' said LB.

'Cool,' said Kelly. She looked over at her bed and let out a long breath.

LB turned around to her. 'You could do an hour's revision?'

'Let me go moisturise, then see how I feel.'

In the attic room, incense was burning, tea lights were flickering, and Amber and Rupert were sitting cross-legged opposite each other, each on their own bed. They had notes in neat piles in front of them.

'And correct!' said Rupert, lowering the page. '*Deich as deich!*' Ten out of ten.

Amber bowed.

'We *shall* go to the ball!' said Rupert. 'I shall get the boy . . .' He tutted. 'Like he's an object! Anyway, he's probably straight and I've totally misread everything, and I have no clue how to even be gay. Maybe he thinks I'm straight. Oh my God. And he's all friends with me because I'm one of the guys, which I obviously am, but . . .' He let out a long breath.

Amber smiled at him. She climbed across her bed and over to his, and they sat side by side, arms linked.

'I'm not sure I like being gay,' said Rupert, eyes on the world beyond the window.

Amber, eyes on his downcast reflection, patted his arm gently. 'I know,' she said. 'I know.' She leaned her head against him, and he leaned his against hers.

27

Kelly walked down the dim corridor to Lockie and Rupert's room. She was dressed in a bathrobe with oversized pockets, and the hood was up. Just as she arrived at the door, it opened, and Réiltín came out, clipboard clutched to her chest. They were both startled. They both waited.

'It's eleven thirty,' said Réiltín.

Kelly nodded. 'I just needed a pen.'

'There were no pens in your room?' said Réiltín. 'LB didn't have any?'

'She was using them all,' said Kelly.

Réiltín smirked. 'I can get you one from the office. Or do you need *all* of them?'

Kelly tried to look past Réiltín's shoulder to Lockie's door.

'You can come with me now,' said Réiltín.

Kelly's eyes flashed with anger. 'Can I not just—'

Réiltín shook her head. 'No.' She gestured for Kelly to

go back to her room. Kelly turned stiffly and started to walk. Réiltín followed her.

'You're a freak,' said Kelly, glancing back, walking on. She gave a dramatic shudder.

When they got to Kelly and LB's door, Réiltín stopped. 'Do you really need a pen? Or—'

'What was your problem back there? With Lockie,' said Kelly.

'I don't have a problem with Lockie,' said Réiltín.

'Then what were you doing in his room?' said Kelly.

'I work here,' said Réiltín.

'Oh, yeah – I forgot,' said Kelly. 'In and out of everyone's rooms. I'd say you love it.' She spun around, opened her door and disappeared inside.

Réiltín walked down the corridor, turned right, and stalled there. Two minutes later, she heard the click of a door opening. She rolled her eyes. She stuck her head out and saw Kelly walking back towards Lockie and Rupert's room. Réiltín ran with the lightest of steps and got to her just as she was about to knock on the door.

'Don't you dare,' hissed Réiltín.

Kelly jumped and turned around.

Réiltín stabbed a finger at her. 'Don't you dare go near him tonight. Just because you don't care about the exam. He does—'

'No, he doesn't,' said Kelly.

'Yes, he does,' said Réiltín.

'You don't know him,' said Kelly.

'I went to school with a girl who hated doing badly in exams,' said Réiltín. 'But do you know what she hated more? Doing badly alone.'

Kelly stared at her. 'Is that thing permanently glued to you?' she said, flicking the clipboard.

'If it was,' said Réiltín, 'could I do this?' She took the clipboard and whacked it hard against the pocket of Kelly's bathrobe. The sound was a dull plink. 'Or this?' said Réiltín, raising it high, then sending it down with a powerful backhand against the other pocket. This time there was the muffled sound of cracking glass.

Kelly stared at her, open-mouthed. She looked down at her right-hand pocket, pulled it out and saw broken glass. 'Oh my God! Psycho!' she said. 'That could have cut me.' She bent down and readjusted her robe.

Réiltín held out an open palm. Kelly looked down at it. 'What?'

'I have to confiscate the alcohol,' said Réiltín.

Kelly glared at her. 'Are you serious? Take it, fine, whatever. Is there anything else you'd like to take belonging to me?'

'What's that supposed to mean?' said Réiltín.

162

'What do you mean?' mocked Kelly. She pushed her face into Réiltín's. 'Do you think I'm stupid? I know what you're doing.'

'I'm not doing anything,' said Réiltín.

Kelly pulled out the bottle from her other pocket and slapped it into Réiltín's hand. 'Bet you're sorry you didn't break this too.'

Réiltín shook her head. 'No.' She raised the bottle high over her shoulder. 'Because then I couldn't do this.' Kelly flinched as Réiltín swung the bottle down hard towards the doorframe, stopping an inch short.

Kelly stared at her.

Réiltín tucked the clipboard under her arm, unscrewed the bottle cap and took a swig of vodka.

'Nutcase,' said Kelly.

Réiltín gave a matter-of-fact shrug.

'Do you really think LB's your friend?' said Kelly. 'I *told* her to go talk to you at the céilí to distract you, because I needed to . . .' She trailed off. 'None of your business what I needed to do. And Rupert's only nice to you because he wants to get with Tadhg.' She shook her head slowly. 'You're being played.' She snorted. 'Like a boring board game.' She turned and walked away.

'Kelly?' said Réiltín. 'I won't tell if you won't tell.'

Kelly looked back. 'Tell what?'

'If you don't tell anyone what I just did,' said Réiltín, 'I won't tell anyone what you just did.'

'I didn't do anything to you,' said Kelly.

'No,' said Réiltín. 'I won't tell anyone that you went down to Lockie's room, wearing nothing but a robe with a bottle of vodka in the pocket. Because you knew that the only way you could ever get him was when he was drunk.'

Réiltín stood where she was until Kelly disappeared into her room. Her heart was pounding, her hands trembling. She filled up the cap of the vodka bottle and knocked back another mouthful. Beside her, the door clicked open a fraction, and Lockie's head appeared.

'That's not true. You're not boring,' he said.

Réiltín's heart lifted. 'Thanks.'

'And there's no way LB would ever do something like that,' said Lockie. He paused. 'What was all the "if I had, I couldn't do this" stuff?'

'Standard security protocol,' said Réiltín. She saluted. 'Sleep safely, sir.'

Lockie reached out for the vodka, gave some eyebrow raises.

'Not happening, sir.'

Réiltín kept the solemn face and demeanour until she was a few feet away, then she turned back and flashed him a grin.

* * *

Kelly stood in the bathroom and carefully stepped out of her robe. She grabbed a hand towel from beside the sink and placed the big pieces of broken glass in it. She shook as many of the little pieces as she could out of the pocket, then gathered up the towel and the bathrobe and shoved them into the bottom of the bathroom cabinet.

She looked in the mirror, and blinked back tears. Réiltín really was a psycho. And there was no one she could tell. The others would kill her for trying to distract Lockie.

PART TWO - PAPER

28

Miss Breathnach sat at the edge of her desk, arms folded, legs crossed at the ankles. A pile of exam papers were stacked beside her. Students were filtering into the classroom and taking their seats. Kelly bounced in, strode to the window and flopped onto a chair. She unzipped her bag, pulled out her pencil case and put it on the desk next to her, to reserve it for LB. Then she pulled her desk a little closer when the teacher was distracted. And did the same for the desks in front and behind. Then she sat back, proud.

LB sprinted towards the classroom, shifting the straps of her backpack, trying to get comfortable. She spotted the college bus up ahead, and saw the driver hopping out, a pencil case in his raised hand, and running up the path after one of the students. LB realised she could slow down a little – they were all going to the same exam. As she walked past the open door of the bus, she paused as a breeze caught the newspaper on the driver's seat, rippling the front page. LB stopped, her heart plummeting. She glanced around, then reached in and slid the paper towards her.

It was her father. And her mother. Plastered across the front page. Under the headline *ON THE ROCKS?*

Instead of going through the front door of the main building, LB ran around the side, tears streaming down her face.

'Lotus Behan! Stop immediately.' LB turned to see Suze, Johnny's wife, standing under a metal fire escape. She was dressed in a long black dress, huge, square, vintage sunglasses, and had a cigarette raised between two fingers.

'Come here,' said Suze.

'Sorry – I can't,' said LB. 'I have to go.'

'Isn't your exam this morning?' said Suze. She took a drag on her cigarette.

LB nodded.

'And wasn't it your door I saw the light shining under at two o'clock in the morning?'

LB nodded.

Suze finished her cigarette, threw down the butt and stamped it out with her boot. 'Don't ever smoke.' She walked over to LB. 'Go to your exam.'

'No!' said LB. 'I can't.' She teared up again.

Suze laid her hands gently on LB's shoulders and looked her in the eye. 'I know why you're crying, OK?'

Lotus head snapped up. 'No, you don't.'

Suze nodded. 'I do. I thought you couldn't have seen anything yet. But here you are.' She looked down at the tabloid in LB's hand. 'You know how it goes – don't believe everything you read. Why would you believe this?'

LB nodded. 'Sorry, but . . . can I just go? I just want to be in my room.'

'Hiding in your room isn't going to change anything,' said Suze. 'You'll just be there, alone, torturing yourself with all kinds of questions that no one can answer. Trust me, you really will be better off with your friends. Even in an exam. Be with other people, your friends, whoever.' She paused. 'How about you call home after the exam? Would that help?'

'Really?' said LB.

'Don't look so surprised,' said Suze. 'It's not a prison.' She glanced over her shoulder at the peeling exteriors of the buildings, the barred windows, the lines of industrial doors and bolts and, beyond them, a horizon of fences. She lit up another cigarette and exhaled a long line of smoke, then turned back to LB. 'Despite all signs to the contrary.'

171

Kelly did a full circle of the college but found no sign of LB. She stood, hot and sweaty, a little distance from the classroom, her head lowered, catching her breath. What the hell was going on with LB? There was no point in doing the exam without her. Kelly hadn't a hope of getting an H-anything without LB. At least if neither of them showed, then neither of them would get to go to the party, and maybe they could figure a way of hitching a ride somewhere they could actually drink. Kelly stood up, and caught a glimpse of movement in the classroom window.

Miss Breathnach was just closing the door when LB arrived back, but she smiled and let her through. LB stopped inside the door, scanning the room for Kelly, but she couldn't see her. The teacher pointed her to a free seat at the back by the window. LB paused, panicked, looking for Kelly again, until it got too awkward.

LB sat down at the only free desk and turned to see Kelly's Boy from the céilí beside her.

'Oh!' they both said at the same time. Then as Miss Breathnach was telling them to turn to page one, they jumped at the sound of hammering on the glass.

Kelly was standing outside, her face red with rage. LB couldn't hear what she was shouting, but she could read her lips.

29

On Friday afternoon, Miss Breathnach stood at the top of the classroom holding a pile of corrected exam papers to her chest. She smiled at everyone as they walked in.

'*We just need you to know we love you. From day one,*' said Rupert, his Irish fluent.

Miss Breathnach laughed. '*The papers are already corrected, Rupert.*'

'Now, I know you all worked hard these past three weeks,' said Miss Breathnach when they all sat down, which is why I'm talking in English to give you a break.'

They all laughed.

'I know this hasn't been easy,' she said. 'So if you didn't get the grade you were hoping for, that does not mean you won't get it in your Leaving Cert. That's ten months away – you've plenty of time. This way you can see which areas still need work.' She put the exam papers down on the desk. 'Now, for those of you who got the H1, it's party night tomorrow night! But if you're one of those who missed out, please don't be disheartened. There'll be other parties, and at least everyone will be home early.' She laughed. 'And I'm sure your friends will step in and know exactly how to cheer you up.'

Kelly walked back to the college, a few feet to the left of the rest of the group, her eyes on the ground ahead.

'Can you imagine,' said Rupert, half-turning to Kelly as he walked, 'what it would have been like if you actually liked or cared about Irish and your result? Or you actually weren't going to crash the party anyway? You could be devastated right now.'

Amber kept her head down to hide her smile.

Kelly bore her eyes into Rupert. 'There's no way I'm going to crash that party like a loser.'

'You'll feel like a winner after a few G and Ts, though,' said Lockie.

Everyone except Kelly laughed.

'I missed the start of the exam!' said Kelly. 'Remember?'

'So those ten minutes you lost at the start,' said Lockie, 'they contained all your Irish.'

Kelly glared at him. 'I was so stressed out about LB!' she said. 'I didn't know where she was!'

Amber dug her fingers into LB's arm. 'That didn't mean you had to go looking for her,' said Amber to Kelly. 'That was a choice you made.'

'What was I supposed to do?' said Kelly. 'I was worried—'

'That you'd have no one to copy from,' said Lockie.

Kelly stopped walking and stood with her hands on her hips. 'How, though, did *you* get a H1?'

'One person's success is another person's bewilderment,' said Rupert.

'I'm not bewildered,' said Kelly.

'OK, you're just doing a really good impression of someone who is,' said Rupert.

'You're all being so horrible,' said Kelly. 'Seriously. Leave me alone. For the whole rest of the time. I'll just see you on Sunday.'

She stormed off. Amber and Rupert exchanged patient looks.

Everyone walked the rest of the way back in silence. When they reached the front entrance of the Lodge, Réiltín appeared on the stone steps. Lockie dropped his bag and raised his arms, triumphant.

Réiltín covered her mouth with her hands and said a muffled 'H1?'

'Yes, ma'am.'

Réiltín squealed, ran down the steps, and threw her

arms around him. He hugged her hard, lifting her off her feet. He set her down gently, then put his arm around her and, turning to the others, said, 'I'd like to dedicate this literally unbelievable achievement to the girl who made it all possible.' He gestured with a sweep of his arm. 'Réiltín Raye Secret Tutor!'

The others gasped, then cheered.

LB ran up the steps. Réiltín politely stepped aside as LB threw her arms around Lockie.

'I'm so happy for you,' said LB. 'Oh my God, sorry for crying! You're amazing. I know how hard it's been, and . . .' She started laughing against his chest and raised her head to look at Réiltín. 'I was about to say, "You're a star"!'

Réiltín laughed. 'Just a little one.'

Rupert went with Amber to her room to celebrate.

'All those runs Lockie wasn't going on,' said Rupert. 'We should have noticed how he'd let himself go.'

Amber laughed. 'It's so hilarious – Lockie and Réiltín.'

'The eyes Kelly was boring into everyone on the way back,' said Rupert. He hopped up and stood at the top of the stairs in a showman stance. '*Kellyvision*,' he said in a voiceover voice. 'Doing something you shouldn't be doing? *Kellyvision*. Saying something you shouldn't be saying? *Kellyvision*. Talking to someone you shouldn't be talking to? *Kellyvision*. Getting grades she hasn't been getting? *Kellyvision*. If you've been affected by any of the issues . . .'

He trailed off and followed Amber's gaze to where Réiltín stood behind him, holding a neat pile of bedlinen.

'Oh – Friday, of course,' said Rupert, taking it from her. 'Thank you.'

'And yours are in your room,' said Réiltín. She looked at both of them. 'I know you're going home on Sunday, so you probably won't bother changing them—'

'We will not,' said Rupert. 'But thank you.'

Réiltín smiled.

Amber leaned out to her. 'Were you in the girls' room? Is LB around?'

'No,' said Réiltín, 'but I bumped into her on the stairs. She said she was going to ask Johnny if she could use the phone.'

'OK,' said Amber.

'Kelly was in the room,' Réiltín offered.

A silence fell.

'Did she say anything?' said Rupert.

'No,' said Réiltín. 'But the Kellyvision was on.'

30

LB was approaching the front desk. There was no sign of Réiltín. She could hear Johnny's voice through the office door behind the desk. Just then, he yanked the door open, his phone in his hand. LB ducked down, out of sight.

'Sorry,' he said into the phone, 'my Bluetooth died. I'm putting you on speaker.'

'Look, Johnny. I'm sorry about last night—'

LB froze, pressed back against the wall. That was Ash's voice on the other end of the phone.

'Kelly . . . she's always had a problem with her emotions,' said Ash.

LB winced, and looked for a way out.

'They're like this wild horse she finds herself on – too late. And the only way the journey ends is when she throws herself off.'

'Or throws someone across a GAA hall,' said Johnny.

Ash laughed. 'I've seen you throw a few people across a dance floor, me included. No one was hurt – that's the main thing.' She paused. 'If she's getting that drunk, it's usually because she's upset about something. Make sure she doesn't show up at that party tomorrow night, OK? She'll already be disappointed with how she got on in the exam, no matter what she says, and if she drinks . . . yada yada yada.'

'I think she's upset about being here in the first place,' said Johnny.

'I know,' said Ash. 'I know. I made her go. I would never have dreamed of sending her to the Gaeltacht. But she reacted so badly when the Behans cancelled their trip . . .'

LB's eyes widened.

'And frankly,' said Ash, 'I was worried that her relationship with LB might suffer, especially if LB was going away with the rest of the gang. Kelly couldn't handle that. She's always been afraid of losing people. She'd never admit it, but it would be her worst nightmare if LB came back closer to one of the others. Even one of the gang. Kelly's just not very good at being on her own.'

'I get it, I get it,' said Johnny. 'And like you said, no one got hurt in a way that turns into a lawsuit. I'd like to turn this madhouse into a spa-house.'

'And does running the college bring in enough?' said Ash.

Johnny walked back into the office. LB made a move to crawl away from the front desk.

'It brings in enough to wine and dine potential investors,' said Johnny.

'Hmm,' said Ash. 'Leave that with me. What are your thoughts on dirty work?'

Johnny paused. *'Céad míle fáilte.'* A thousand welcomes.

LB dived, scrambled and slid for the door through to the hallway, Johnny's helpful laughter drowning out her escape.

LB's heart was pounding, her head swirling. What the hell just happened? And Johnny? And "dirty work"? She ran up the stairs to the first floor and met Réiltín on the landing.

'Did you get hold of your parents?' said Réiltín.

'I think Johnny was in the office on a call,' said LB. 'I couldn't really hear him.'

'Just the general boom,' said Réiltín. 'Well, just come back later, OK? He's going out in a little while.'

'Thanks,' said LB. She was turning to walk away when Réiltín stopped her.

'I . . . I saw about your dad,' said Réiltín. 'And mom, obviously. And . . . well, I didn't know whether to say anything—'

'No, it's OK,' said LB.

'I just wanted to say I'm sorry you're dealing with that,' said Réiltín.

'Thanks,' said LB. 'Mom probably won't pick up when I call later, anyway. Because of the two-hour call we had the other night, and me having a meltdown . . .' She gave a small smile. 'I know my parents have a lot more important things going on, but they're always who I call with good news. Even though it's not an *exam* exam . . . I did put in the work, and—'

'OK,' said Réiltín. 'Look at me. Tell me . . . what just happened today?'

'Oh my God! I got a H1 in Irish!!!' LB screamed.

'Oh my God! Congratulations!!!' said Réiltín.

They both jumped up and down, screaming together, and LB flung her arms about Réiltín, and Réiltín flung her arms around LB, and the two of them were bouncing around the floor screaming together when Kelly walked up the stairs, and they both sprung apart.

Lockie was in his room on a Zoom call with his therapist.

'Obviously, the timing for you with everything has not been easy over the past three weeks,' said his therapist. 'And, still, you reached out for help when you needed it.'

'It's so weird,' said Lockie. 'Like, if someone told me last year that I'd be in the Gaeltacht in August, learning Irish – like studying it properly with Réiltín Raye, who

I have a meltdown in front of, and . . .'

'Life is full of surprises.'

'I know,' said Lockie.

'And you got the result you wanted in the exam—'

'Yeah! Well, there was nothing else to do here except study.'

The therapist smiled. 'Take the win. You worked hard. You deserve it.'

Lockie shrugged. 'No, like, I'm proud of myself. I am.'

'How did that feel to say?'

'Messed up.'

'You're allowed to be proud of yourself, Marcus. We don't have to be who someone tells us we are.'

'Unless it's awesome.'

His therapist laughed. 'OK, Marcus, we're going to have to wrap it up there for today. And we'll talk next week. I'll send you the link. You'll be home then.'

Lockie nodded. 'Yeah, the room won't be as nice.'

The therapist laughed. 'Enjoy the party. And take it easy on the drinking, if you can.' He paused. 'You know what the next day can do for the head. And I don't mean the hangover.'

LB left the landing and walked with Kelly down to their room.

'Yeah, definitely, congratulations,' said Kelly.

'Thanks,' said LB.

'I'm really happy for your results,' said Kelly. 'I really am . . . but will you all be normal when we get back to Dublin?' She laughed.

LB laughed with her. 'What do you mean, "normal"? Not being "boring bitches"?'

Kelly laughed. 'I'm actually going to be the boring bitch tomorrow night.' She stopped walking. 'OK, I know – how about we just stay in? You and me? We do face masks, I'll do your nails.' She paused. 'It's going to be a crap party anyway.'

LB looked at her. 'Maybe.' She smiled, and put her arms around Kelly. She squeezed her tight and held her in a long hug. 'You know you're my best friend in the whole world? And you always will be and I love you and you're gorgeous and you're so much fun and you make me laugh and . . .'

'So will you stay in with me?' said Kelly as LB was gently releasing her.

32

Amber was sitting in her room, on her bed, shuffling cards. Rupert appeared on the stairs, and Amber jumped. Rupert looked at the cards, and looked at Amber's face. He came up the stairs and sat down beside her.

'Now,' he said, 'delicate topic of conversation because I love you. But I think, maybe, we need to have a chat about...'

They both looked down. All three decks were open, and there were lines of cards laid out. Amber looked up at Rupert. 'I know, I know,' she said. 'I know. I'm doing way too many readings. I know.'

'And there's nothing wrong with that,' said Rupert. He paused. 'OK, backtrack. I think there is, a little bit. I'm just so used to thinking that there's nothing wrong with anything you do.'

'Aw, Rupe,' said Amber. Tears welled in her eyes.

'Maybe all these readings are a little too much,' said Rupert. 'You probably can't see it, but I think they kind of affect your mood—'

'But in a good way sometimes,' said Amber.

Rupert nodded. 'Of course. But . . . I don't want to ask you how many you're doing a day, because that's awful, but how about I ask you whether you maybe think you're doing too many?'

Amber nodded, tears spilling down her face. 'It's just . . .' She shrugged. 'Just . . .'

Rupert took her hands in his, and held them firm, and waited.

Amber wiped away tears. 'I'm just so used to being told that everything's going to go wrong.'

Rupert nodded. 'And you just want to know your future is safe.'

Amber broke down in tears. She moved over to Rupert and he held her in his arms as she cried.

'Thanks,' she said into his chest.

He held her there, laying his hand gently on her head. 'Your future will always be bright with me, Ambs.'

LB left Kelly in their room, crossed the corridor to 3A, and called up the stairs to Amber .

'Come up,' said Amber. 'Rupe's here.'

'Hey,' said LB. She turned to Rupert. 'I thought nobody was allowed to touch them.' She pointed to the three oracle decks stacked in his hands.

'I'm just . . . borrowing them,' said Rupert.

'I'm addicted to them and he's taking them out of my reach,' said Amber. 'I'm going to be releasing them tomorrow night at the ritual, he just said.'

'Just a suggestion, and not forever,' said Rupert, 'and actually, what I was saying was that you should release your fear of the future. Which will be helped by not having access to it in card format.'

The girls laughed.

'That's true – you did say "fear of the future",' said Amber.

'Everything I say is the truth!' said Rupert.

'That's true too,' said Amber. LB nodded in agreement.

'Then I have to think about what I want to release,' said LB.

Rupert raised the decks. 'It's only for two days,' he said to Amber. 'Unless I get addicted.'

'Don't touch her cards!' said LB.

Rupert turned to LB. 'Can you please tell our beautiful Amber that nothing bad is going to happen?'

LB's eyes widened. 'Yes, of course. Totally.' She flopped down on the bed next to Amber's and flung her arms back over her head. She stared at the ceiling. Who could she tell about what had happened at the front desk?

Not Kelly, because then Kelly would know her mother was talking to Johnny about her, and if Kelly then told Ash, then Ash would know precisely which conversation LB had overheard.

Not Amber and Rupert, because ... how afraid would you be of the future if you knew you had forty-eight hours left in an asylum with someone who was happy to do dirty work?

Could she tell Lockie? Would he confront Johnny? He could, so not Lockie. And definitely not Réiltín, who worked for Johnny. Not even her parents, who were too busy with their own problems, and who were friends with Johnny anyway ...

'What's going through your tiny mind?' said Rupert, watching her.

LB sat up. 'Nothing.'

'How's Kelly after her stormage?' said Rupert. He narrowed his eyes. 'What level of tension are we at?'

LB smiled. 'It's fine, we hugged . . . but she wants me to hang out with her tomorrow night, not go to the party, have a spa night in with her.'

'Oh my God,' said Rupert. 'Is she trying to blame you for the exam thing?'

'I do feel bad. But no . . . she hasn't said that.'

'You're not to blame,' said Amber.

'But *you* feel bad?' said Rupert. 'Oh my God, LB.'

Amber looked at her. 'You're allowed to tell the truth about her,' she said. 'You're allowed to say, "Kelly is guilting me about tomorrow night," and not feel mean about it. It's true. She is trying to guilt you.'

LB looked at her. 'It feels mean.' She shrugged. 'And maybe I'm reading too much into things.'

'No, you're not,' said Rupert immediately.

'It still feels mean,' said LB.

'OK – forget that,' said Rupert. 'How about this? You're allowed to be happy when Kelly is not. You're allowed to have fun with other people when Kelly can't. You're allowed—'

'To do anything you want to do!' said Amber, slamming her fist down on the bed.

LB's eyes went wide.

'Seriously!' said Amber. 'Say to her, "I've got my own stuff to deal with right now; I've been working my ass off; I just scored a H1—"'

'Or,' said Rupert, 'say, "Enjoy spa night for one. The End."'

LB smiled. 'But she'll be here on her own, and she's not into that . . .'

'I say, let the lunatic run the asylum!' said Rupert.

'So what am I meant to do?' said LB.

'Precisely what I said,' said Rupert.

'Kelly can't stop you going tomorrow night,' said Amber. 'Do. Not. Let her!'

33

At ten o'clock, LB came back down to the office to try to call home again. There was no answer.

She tried her dad's phone, and he picked up.

'Suze!' he said. 'Is that you? What the—'

'Dad? It's LB!'

Silence.

'Dad! It's me – LB!'

'Jesus . . . LB, baby. Sorry . . . sorry.'

He sounded drunk.

'What's going on, Dad? said LB. 'I was talking to Mom.'

'Yeah?'

'Dad, you do know I saw the papers? *Days ago.* I left you voicemails.'

'It's a madhouse here . . . it's a madhouse there!'

LB smiled. 'Stop. It's not funny.'

'It's not funny, but . . . it's just the papers, LB.'

Silence.

'Lotus Blossom—'

'Don't. Where's Mom?'

'She's gone over to . . . er, to one of the girls. She's with the girls.'

'What?' said LB.

'Hanging with the girls . . . !' said her dad. 'Drinking Prosecco.'

LB paused. 'Are you two breaking up, Dad? Are you? Just tell me. Are you?'

'Listen to me. Listen to me, sweetheart. Sweetheart – no one's breaking up. No one's doing anything. Your dad's drunk. Your mom probably is too. Nothing you haven't seen before—'

LB rolled her eyes.

'My little worrier,' said her dad. 'Stop. All is well. We've been here before. Lies, lies, all lies. We don't talk about stories in the papers, you and me. We know they're not the truth.'

'I don't *know* what the truth is any more,' said LB.

A silence stretched between them.

'Promise?' said LB.

'Of course I promise.' Her dad paused. 'Oh . . . that's your mom back. I think.'

LB could hear him call out: 'Trish! Trish! It's—' In the background, LB could hear the click of her mother's heels on the tiles, then the snap of her voice as she replied: 'I don't even want to look at you right now.'

LB slammed the phone down.

Kelly was sitting at the dressing table, setting it up like a treatment room, when LB burst in the door. Kelly jumped, knocked a bottle of nail polish onto the carpet, then whipped it back up.

'Thank God it wasn't open,' she said, scowling. She looked up, then saw LB's tears.

'Oh no – what happened?' said Kelly. She went to LB, brought her over to the bed, and they sat down together.

LB shook her head. 'Dad's drunk, says it's all lies, says Mom's at her friends', drinking Prosecco – hello? – and then Mom walks in and says to him, "I don't even want to look at you right now." And it was horrible and I just hung up. I don't know what's going on.'

Kelly sighed. 'Do you want to check it out online?' she said. 'Because I walked by Lockie's room earlier, and it totally sounded like he was on a Zoom call, which means he has to have the Wi-Fi code . . . and . . . and we could look up the story.'

'Ew. No,' said LB. 'That would literally be like, "Here

are even more lies to think about and loads of strangers' opinions on them."'

'OK, will I look?' said Kelly. 'And I can do the usual – filter out the really bad stuff.'

'Oh my God! What do you think it's going to be?' said LB.

'Nothing!' said Kelly. 'Just . . . well, we'll find out.' She shrugged. 'If they're breaking up—'

'Yeah, but they're not! Dad said.'

'But he was drunk,' said Kelly. 'And your mom was "at a friend's".'

'But she came back!' said LB.

'And acted like she wanted to kill him,' said Kelly, rising from the bed. 'I'm just going to go and have a quick look. OK?'

LB nodded reluctantly. 'OK.'

Lockie was sitting on his bed, laptop closed, debating opening it. It's not like anyone would care now. They were done. They were going home in two days.

There was a knock on the door. 'Who is it?'

'Rupety-doop.'

Lockie laughed. Rupert came in, arm in arm with Amber.

'Did you tell your dad the bad news?' said Rupert. 'That he's wrong about you?'

Lockie laughed. 'No, I want to be face to face for that one.'

'For what one?' said Kelly, walking in the door, slinking past Rupert and Amber. She looked around. 'I seriously don't know what happened to all of you,' she went on. 'I was saying to LB, I'm really happy for your results, I really am, but will you be normal when we get back to Dublin? Please?'

'Will you?' said Lockie.

'Never,' said Kelly. She walked over and sat beside him on his bed. 'No judgement, but I know you've got the Wi-Fi code, and—'

'Nope,' said Lockie.

Kelly shook her head. 'Not your final answer.' She turned to the others. 'He had Wi-Fi all along.'

Anger flickered in Lockie's eyes. 'No – three times. For private reasons.'

'Clare,' said Kelly.

Lockie ignored her.

'I just want to look something up,' said Kelly.

'What?' said Lockie.

'I'm not joking,' said Kelly. 'It's about LB. She's freaking out about her dad and the story in the paper. She thinks her parents are about to split up. Her dad's not making sense, her mom hates him, and obviously, because we're

195

currently living in an *asylum* where our phones have been locked away from us, we don't know what actually *is* being said. So I just want to –' she gestured towards the laptop – 'you know – put LB's mind at rest—'

Rupert looked at her. 'If it *was* the 1800s, I'd understand how you might not know how the internet works, but I think we all now know that, whatever you find, it isn't going to put anyone's mind at rest, it really isn't . . .'

'You just want to know all the juicy details,' said Lockie.

'I just want to help her,' said Kelly. 'OK?'

'Why don't you tell her you looked it up and just couldn't find anything?' said Amber. 'Let her at least try to enjoy tomorrow night.'

'But just – look, I don't want to say, "Oh, there's nothing, LB!" and then she goes online when we get our phones back, which will be *Sunday*—'

'I don't think she'll do that,' said Amber. 'I think she'll wait until she's home. And at least she'll have some hope of hearing the truth then.'

'But what if she doesn't wait till then?' said Kelly. 'What if there's this massive story we could have all warned her about?'

Lockie opened his laptop and started typing. 'Fine.'

They all went over and gathered around him.

The first headline they saw was: *IS THIS IT?* There

was a photo of LB's smiling parents with a Photoshopped rip down the middle, and a circle with *Are Antsy and Trix over?* And, underneath, *Has rock royalty's crown toppled?*

Everyone exchanged glances.

'It's so funny seeing "Trix" when you know her as Trish,' said Kelly. 'She had to have a cool name to keep up with Antsy.' She reached over Lockie and scrolled through more stories.

After five minutes, she stood up and shook her head.

'So, let me get this straight,' said Kelly. 'I go back to LB and . . . Lie number one: "I was totally wrong about Lockie having the Wi-Fi code." Lie number two: "Lockie was just talking out loud to a video he had downloaded before we even came to college!" Lie number three: "It's all going to be fine."'

They all nodded.

'Yeah, that's way better,' said Kelly. 'Way better than "looks like your parents *are* splitting up and FYI your dad has a secret love child".'

Rupert gave her a steadying look. 'That love child thing was a tiny few lines in some sneaky forum, not in the actual papers. Let's not supersize it yet.'

Kelly nodded. 'Until we find out more.'

34

Réiltín sat at the front desk wishing she hadn't gone up to let LB know her dad was on the phone. But it was Antsy. She couldn't just tell him, 'Oh, hello Antsy slash Mr Behan – she didn't even know which – no, sorry, you can't talk to your daughter.' Réiltín had read most of the stories online about him earlier. The news was so awful if it was true. But at least she was able to fill LB in on most of it before she made it to the office. All she could hear now was sobbing. She couldn't hear any of the details, but whatever it was that LB's dad had said to her when she came on the call had made LB burst into tears. Since then she'd been sobbing through most of it. Réiltín didn't really want to be there, but she had to stay in case Johnny came back. And in case LB needed someone to talk to after.

LB was sitting on the floor in Johnny's office, her back against his desk, her cheeks hot and damp with tears. Her breath was shaky with sobs.

'LB – LB, baby – calm down,' said her father.

'How am I supposed to calm down?' cried LB. 'You cheated on Mom!'

'Not exactly . . .'

'Oh my God, what?'

'I mean . . . your mom and I . . . we—'

'Oh my God – stop,' said LB. 'I don't want to know. I don't want to have this conversation.'

'I'm sorry you saw the paper. I didn't want you to stumble across—'

LB looked around Johnny's office. 'Oh my God. This is why I'm here! Is this why I'm here?'

Silence.

'Is this why I'm here?' she said again.

'You should see outside our gates,' said her dad. 'I couldn't have you—'

'So you knew this was coming, and you just made a decision – ship LB off?'

'With your friends—'

'What? You shipped them off too?'

'No, I meant . . . this was an opportunity – your Irish teacher – with him leaving—'

'So you "encouraged" all the other parents, did you? Talked it up? Said you'd pull the strings, looked like a hero? Oh my God. Who *does* that? And who can ever say no to Antsy?'

'Come on, LB – this was good for you and the guys. I wasn't sending you to a workhouse.'

'No – an asylum!'

'Come on – I knew you'd think that was fun if you found out.'

LB paused. 'It kind of was, but . . .'

'Look, I knew you'd be safe, and you'd be with your friends,' said her dad, 'and I knew you'd look after each other . . .'

LB broke down and spoke through sobs. 'But . . . I just . . . want . . . you . . . to look after me.'

Rupert was sitting on the bed with Lockie's laptop. Kelly was standing by the door, ready to leave.

'Poor LB,' she said.

'It still could be lies, all lies,' said Rupert.

Kelly nodded over to him. 'Are you still searching?'

'Of course I am!' said Rupert, his eyes narrowing as he scanned the screen. He paused, and did a dramatic double-take. 'Ooh, did we all know that Réiltín's mom used to be a stylist . . . and she worked with Antsy?'

Kelly rushed over. Rupert enlarged a photo. 'Antsy, Caruvi – that's her mom's name, right? – rest of the band, Johnny and Suze Metcalfe at Le Petit something . . .'

'Oh my God, that's Johnny Owner!' said Kelly. 'He was hot.'

'And,' said Rupert, 'his attic wife was, at least, alive in . . .' He squinted at the screen. 'In 2003.' He sat back and looked up at Kelly. 'Think that might explain the rumours you heard about Réiltín's framed poster art, don't you? Doesn't your mom have some too? Aren't they given as gifts?'

Kelly got up and walked over to the door. 'I better get back to LB.' She paused. 'Why wouldn't Réiltín have said to LB that her mom used to work for her dad?'

Amber nodded. 'I know – they get on so well.'

Kelly's eyes sparked with anger. 'Actually,' she said, 'Réiltín probably didn't know. Her mother was probably just freelance. It wasn't like she was *staff*.'

'Or,' said Rupert, 'maybe she did tell her. Do you all tell each other *everything*?'

'Yeah,' said Lockie. 'You're all so obsessed with knowing stuff about each other and who knows what and who cares?' He turned to Rupert. 'Like, Rupert, do you know what jocks I'm wearing today?'

'I do!' said Rupert. 'I laid out your entire outfit on the bed.'

Everyone laughed.

'Seriously, though,' said Lockie, 'just calm down, everyone.'

'I am calm!' said Kelly.

'Regardless,' said Rupert, looking at her, 'do you really think that LB would find you particularly receptive to conversations about Réiltín?'

Kelly laughed. 'OK, no. Not unless they're about her dropping off the face of the earth.'

35

On Saturday morning, LB lay curled in bed, staring at the bird-print wallpaper, finding all the bright pink ones. Her pillow was so damp from tears she had flipped it over. She heard the click of the door catch and the soft *swish* it made as it slid open across the carpet.

LB rolled over and saw Kelly, her foot wedging the door open, bending down and picking up a tray from the floor in the corridor. 'I have croissants and Danishes and coffee and juice and fruit salad and—'

LB propped herself up on her elbow. 'Oh my God – you're serious.'

'Of course I'm serious!' said Kelly. 'Imagine coming in announcing all this food and then being like, "Ha! I have nothing!" Worst. Friend. Ever.'

LB smiled. 'Thanks.' She sat up and leaned back on the pillows.

Kelly slid the tray across the bed to her, and sat on the other side of it, stuffing an extra pillow behind her back. 'How are you now?' said Kelly.

LB looked at her. 'Rubbish.'

Kelly nodded. 'I know. When my dad left . . . not that your dad's leaving . . . What I was trying to say last night was . . .'

'It's not the same,' said LB. 'Sorry, but it's not.'

'No, I know,' said Kelly, 'but what I mean is . . . it's hard when . . . when you . . .' She burst into tears. 'It's hard when you don't have your dad in your life.'

LB was startled by the sudden tears. 'Oh no,' she said, pushing the tray aside, wriggling out from under the covers, and clambering over to Kelly. She put her arms around her and could feel the stiffness of her body. She pulled away gently, then reached over and pulled some tissues from the box on the bedside table.

'I never knew how hard that was for you,' said LB, handing them to her.

Kelly nodded, sobbing.

'At least you have BBF,' said LB.

Kelly smiled through her tears. 'Best Bonus Father . . . *everrr*. No, I know. It's just . . .' She let out a breath. 'I don't know . . . I think that whatever's going on with your mom and dad has really triggered me.'

In the garden next to the kitchen, Rupert settled himself on his folded-up college hoodie and leaned back against the trunk of the oak tree. He opened his poetry book to one of his favourite poems. *Hidden Flame*, by John Dryden. He knew the words by heart since he'd met Tadhg. Rupert paused when he heard a car pulling up. It stopped by the path to the kitchen. Rupert watched as Tadhg got out and walked around to the boot.

'Tadhg!' called Rupert, snapping the book closed.

Tadhg looked up, and smiled when he saw him. 'Rupert! Or should I say Master Irish? Beach party for you tonight!'

Rupert nodded. 'Yes. Will you be there?' He backtracked on the eager tone. 'In any official capacity?'

'What – you mean to serve you refreshments?' said Tadhg.

Rupert gasped. 'No – I meant . . .'

Tadhg laughed. 'No, I'm not on official duty tonight.'

Rupert nodded. Silence descended.

'Will you be working in the morning?' said Rupert. 'Our last breakfast?'

'No way,' said Tadhg. 'I never work the morning after my night off.'

Rupert nodded. 'Good plan. Good plan. So . . . well . . . I guess we'll say our . . . I'll say my goodbye now.'

Tadhg looked Rupert in the eye in a way no one had ever looked him in the eye before, or in a way he had never allowed anyone to.

'*Dead Poets Society*!' said Tadhg, pointing to him.

Rupert took a step back, lowered his eyes to his yellow T-shirt and red shorts with a black belt. 'No one got it this morning!' he said. 'NO ONE!' He held up his poetry book. 'Even with this!'

'They probably weren't expecting you to dress as the poster, though.'

'I'm working with a limited wardrobe,' said Rupert.

'What will you be dressed as tonight,' said Tadhg, 'so I can find you on the beach?'

Rupert stared at him. 'A lighthouse.'

Amber was sitting on her bed, her suitcase empty and open beside her. She reached over to the bedside cabinet, pulled the top drawer open but just let her hand rest there, as she continued to sit staring at the wall opposite. She looked around the room, weird and ancient and flowery, and realised she felt more at home there than she ever had in her own bedroom. She slid the top drawer closed, bent down and opened the bottom one, the drawer she'd kept her oracle decks in before Rupert had 'borrowed' them. She just wanted to know what would happen when she got home. If she read her cards, she could get a new beginning card or a fresh start card or a new mother card ... Her breath caught. Tears welled in her eyes. And she didn't know if she felt bad for her mother or for herself. But she did know that there was one person who never made her feel bad – Rupert, her joy. Rupert, who only ever wanted what was best for her. She smiled and wiped her eyes and closed the drawer.

Tadhg pushed backwards through the door, hefting a box of groceries. He walked down the hallway into the kitchen, where Réiltín was waiting. He gave her a huge smile and started unpacking the top items from the box.

'Who even are you?' he said, tilting the box towards her to reveal the items still inside – bottles of Heineken, cans of gin and tonic, a litre bottle of Absolut Vodka, and litre bottles of soft drinks.

'It's really for the others,' said Réiltín, shrugging. 'Like, congratulations! I'm on duty.'

Tadhg handed her a small backpack. 'To transfer them to Lockie's room.'

'Thanks,' said Réiltín, starting to load up the bag.

Tadhg glanced at the clock on the kitchen wall. It was three o'clock. 'Maybe wait until six, just to be on the safe side.'

Réiltín frowned, and paused what she was doing.

'I'm serious,' said Tadhg. 'What if he gets drunk?'

'He's not going to get drunk,' said Réiltín. 'He'd know I'd get in trouble.'

'Good!' said Tadhg. 'That's all I care about.'

Réiltín zipped the backpack closed.

'You should have one drink later,' said Tadhg. 'Like, congratulations to *you*! For surviving three weeks with your arch nemesis. You made it. You're alive!'

Réiltín raised an eyebrow. 'It's not over yet.'

Rupert sprinted up to Amber's room to deliver the news of Tadhg's attendance at the party.

'So,' said Rupert. 'I need you on standby as chaperone.'

Amber looked at him.

'Well, not so much on standby,' said Rupert, 'as stand-right-by me and never leave.'

'Um . . . why?' said Amber.

'Oh my God!' said Rupert. 'Chaperones. How in *all* good period drama love stories—'

'They introduce the *wrong* suitor,' said Amber. 'The mismatch!' She shook her head. 'The *alone* stuff with the *true* love is where all the action happens.'

'Action?' said Rupert, recoiling, faux-disgusted. 'I want to sit with my hands on my knees, back straight, eyes averted—'

'Fine!' said Amber. 'I'll do it, maybe from a safe distance – but only if you let me march you up that rock and stand over you as you write the words *I release fear –*' she narrowed her eyes at Rupert's blank face – '*of kissing boys and liking it.*'

Rupert recoiled again.

Amber laughed. 'What was the plan? Meet Tadhg at the party and . . . what?'

Rupert turned to her. '. . . Put human shields between us until departure.'

'The End?' said Amber. She rolled her eyes.

'A tragic ending, I know,' said Rupert. He shrugged in a gesture of resignation. 'But sometimes . . .'

'No, no, no,' said Amber. '*There's* your mismatch. Two things that absolutely do not go together: "tonight" and "tragic ending".'

PART THREE -
KILLERS

36

Amber stood in front of the mirror, hair brushed, no make-up, just a slick of lip balm. She went to her rucksack and unzipped one of the side pockets where she kept a small backpack. Wrong pocket. She hadn't used it in ages. She went to the other side, unzipped that one, and pulled out the backpack. She shook it. It was heavier than it should have been for an empty bag. When she opened it, her eyes widened. She pulled out the little matte black box with the red writing. She got goosebumps. She remembered the line on the front, read it again: THE FUTURE IS IN YOUR HANDS. Her Rock Paper Scissors oracle deck, the one Kelly had got her when they'd been camping. Or mini deck, actually. The cards were tiny. Small enough to fit in your pocket. If you were desperate.

* * *

Rupert, bare-chested, a towel wrapped around his waist, stood in front of the mirror at the bathroom sink. *My hair is magnificent. And I look terrified. Those things should be mutually exclusive.* He raised his fingers to his hair, then stopped himself. *It's the terror I have to fix here!* He looked himself in the eye.

'Rupert Gore-Graves,' he said out loud, 'tell me now: what is it you're afraid of?' He waited. *Boys* was the answer that came into his mind. 'Excuse me?' said Rupert out loud. 'That's ridiculous! You are friends with boys, and you talk with boys every day. Next question: what are you really afraid of?' *Being gay* was the answer that came this time – quicker than the first one. 'Not. Helpful,' said Rupert. 'NOT helpful.' He paused. 'No follow-up questions for now!' and he turned with speed and walked out into the bedroom.

'Look at you,' he said to his outfit, laid out neatly on the bed. 'See how I have prepared my hair for you.'

'It was just saying it would love that,' said Lockie, popping up from the floor beside his bed.

Rupert gasped, clutched his towel and staggered backwards. 'Why were you hiding?'

'I come in peace,' said Lockie, raising his hands. He waved the shoe that was in one of them.

'What are you pairing those with?' said Rupert.

'These cheeky little numbers,' said Lockie, standing up and gesturing to all the drinks. 'Minus the cans Kelly headed off with.'

Kelly was sitting on the dressing table in Room 1, her bare feet up on the stool, gesturing with a can of gin and tonic to the cosmetics display beside her. 'Look at it!' she said.

LB glanced up. 'What time is it?'

'Nearly time for you to abandon me,' said Kelly. 'And my five remaining cans.'

LB groaned. 'You're not going to drink all those, are you? Just on your own here?'

'Yes, Mom!' said Kelly. 'Come back to the room! Have some too! Take little breaks!'

'Do I look OK?' said LB.

'For a traitor?' said Kelly. 'Yes.' She smiled. 'You're perfect. But I hate you. Don't leave me all on my own.'

'I'm sorry,' said LB, 'I need this. I've got a lot of stuff going on. I've worked really hard for this, and I just . . . I just want to have some fun. What time is it really?'

'Six,' said Kelly.

'What?' said LB. 'Where's Amber? I thought she was coming down.' She hopped up.

'I hope she's OK,' said Kelly.

'Why wouldn't she be?' said LB.

Kelly shrugged. 'I don't know. It's Amber.'

'Who's been in the best form ever,' said LB.

'Yeah,' said Kelly, 'but who knows what's going on behind closed creepy-attic doors?'

'Nothing, probably!' said LB. 'She's probably just getting her kit together for later.'

Kelly rolled her eyes. 'Oh, yeah. The ritual. I love Amber, I do. But . . .'

'Don't be mean,' said LB.

'I release being mean,' said Kelly.

Johnny was in the hallway in front of Réiltín, taking a long swig from a bottle of Heineken. 'Hair of the dog.'

Réiltín frowned.

'Have you never heard that expression?' said Johnny. 'Hair of the dog that bit you? Haven't even heard it from me, repeatedly?' He raised his bottle. 'The drink you drink to cure your hangover of the previous night.' He shook his head. 'Sadly, I need the hair of all the dogs. Now, I know I've given you lots of jobs tonight. And I appreciate all your hard work. But enjoy yourself if you can. Oh, and make sure everyone has their hoodie for the photo. I'll be there, obviously, but as overlord. Other than that, do some low-key spot checks for anyone who looks like they're not fit to be around open water, open flames and open opportunities. What else? Oh, yes – intermittent checks on Kelly Warner, that she's still in her room and (a) not sneaking out to the party, and (b) not sneaking out anywhere else either.'

'Are you serious?' said Réiltín.

'Yes!' said Johnny. 'You squeeze the last bit of power out of this job. Plus I spoke to Mammy Warner, who, after the céilí fiasco was adamant that her daughter should not be allowed out tonight. She's into "teaching" moments. All she needs now is a daughter who's into "learning" moments. Personally, I wouldn't give a fiddler's what Ms Kelly Warner gets up to tonight. I wouldn't give her the satisfaction of a boundary to cross. But after that phone call from Mammy Warner . . . She's a tough woman, by the way, speaking of rabid dogs.'

Réiltín nodded. 'No problem.' She felt a tiny flicker of glee at being Kelly Warner's jailer.

37

Rupert left the post-promo-shot crowd as it began to disperse, and walked across the beach and up the steps to the small car park by the dunes. He hid behind the public recycling bins, pulled off his college hoodie, and pushed it gently through the hole in the clothes bank.

'You're going to a better home,' said Rupert.

LB and Amber stood on the beach, looking out at the sea. The tide was in, the sun was beaming, and the sky was a bright blue.

'Looks like about seventy students made the grade,' said Amber, looking around the groups gathered on the beach.' She looked at LB. 'Kelly didn't come for the photo.'

LB shook her head. 'I still feel really bad about leaving her behind.'

'Yeah, well, don't,' said Amber.

Rupert jogged over to them, smoothing down his top. 'Freedom.'

'LB,' said Amber, 'is still feeling bad about Kelly.'

Rupert looked at them. 'We all know she's going to show up on the beach later, though, right? She just hasn't gone through enough cans yet.'

The girls exchanged glances. 'Why were we thinking she was going to stay in this time?' said Amber.

'You can't keep a bad Kelly down,' said Rupert. 'Even when she was a child. Didn't Ash ground her for something one summer when she was little, and Kelly just rocks up at the party anyway?'

'It wasn't "one summer",' said LB. 'That was at *that* party! In the villa! My tenth birthday. With—'

'The blood!' said Amber and Rupert at the same time.

'God,' said LB, 'it would be great if you had a better memory of that day.'

'But I do,' said Rupert. 'Especially after I've been reminded of the location. Kelly was banned from your treasure hunt because Ash caught her doing something – sneaking a look at the clues, I think. Parenting fail, Ash, because you did not stop that girl's "curious" ways. In both senses of the word.'

Amber nodded. 'Yeah, and Kelly came down anyway. And Ash definitely brings her with us to the fairground,' said Amber.

'No consequences,' said Rupert. 'This is the problem.'

'What fairground?' said LB.

'After Jeremy fell. Then it was all "party over", and then Ash came to the rescue, piled us in the car and took us to some tiny little French fairground as a consolation prize.'

'I literally do not remember that,' said LB. 'I just thought we stayed hanging around the house.'

'With the greatest respect,' said Rupert, 'can we please have some conversations that do not include Kelly's wild wayfarer ways? We'll all see her on the beach later.' He looked across to where Johnny was standing by a pile of stacked wood and a barbecue lighter.

'Let the bonfire commence!' said Rupert.

Later, Réiltín walked along the beach, looking like she was just one of the staff chilling at the party, but performing a general scout for Johnny. She could hear raised voices from a group of about twelve guys standing by the rocks. She walked on a subtle diagonal to get closer. Maybe they were just loud, and not having an argument that was about to kick off. Suddenly one of them exploded backwards out of the group onto the sand. He scrambled back up and lunged at the guy who'd pushed him. Réiltín ran towards them to break it up, but the fight had already started to tumble in her direction. Now, some of them were throwing punches, more were getting knocked back onto the sand.

'Guys!' said Réiltín, running as close as she could get. None of them noticed her. None of them heard her. Suddenly she was pushed backwards, and when she tried to go in again she found herself being pulled in further. She closed her eyes and covered her head with her arms, and suddenly she was being hooked around the waist, and hoisted up in the air. She opened her eyes and saw sand and a man's bare leg and realised she'd been thrown over someone's shoulder. When she was away from the crowd, her saviour set her down on safe ground.

There was a scattering of groups nearby and a few people started to cheer. Réiltín just stood there, her hands over her mouth, eyes smiling up at Lockie.

Then they burst out laughing.

'Oh God,' he said, 'that was . . .' He started laughing harder. 'It was . . . like watching pinball.' His voice went so high at the end that Réiltín was bent double laughing, and eventually they had to sit down on the sand to catch their breath.

'Thank you,' she said, eventually. 'Thank you.'

Lockie tapped a fist lightly on her knee. 'We all need little stars.'

They turned to each other and smiled.

Amber and LB were standing at a distance, watching. They both turned, smiling, to each other at the same time.

'It's hilarious – the two of them,' said LB. 'It's really sweet.'

'They're so chill,' said Amber.

Someone startled them as she sidled up. She pushed her head out of her college hoodie like a tortoise. Kelly's eyes sparkled with mischief. 'Best disguise ever,' she said, gesturing to LB and Amber and all the other girls standing around, all similarly bare-legged and swamped in hoodies that fell to their knees.

'What the hell, Lockie and Réiltín?' said Kelly next, and she pointed towards Lockie and Réiltín with her bottle. 'Seriously. It's creeping me out.'

'Why?' said Amber. 'You're done with him. He's done with you.'

'The End!' said Rupert darting up beside them. 'I told you she'd show.'

'Lockie wasn't "done with me",' said Kelly. 'He wanted a relationship. I didn't. The End.'

'Oh, good,' said Rupert. 'So nothing anyone is doing over in that cosy corner is hurting anyone.'

'I thought he was supposed to be all heartbroken over Clare,' said Kelly.

'Oh, he is,' said Rupert. 'What you are seeing in front of you is a heartbroken man who's feeling a little relief because a friend is being kind to him.'

'What's that supposed to mean?' said Kelly. '*We're* his friends. *We're* kind to him.'

'OK – you are borderline never kind to him,' said Amber.

'What?' said Kelly. 'I'm always kind to him.' She refocused her attention on Lockie and Réiltín. 'I just don't get it.'

'That doesn't it make it wrong,' said Rupert.

Kelly's head spun towards him but got trapped inside her hood. By the time she wriggled out, Rupert was walking away backwards. 'Drinks all round!' he said.

38

When Rupert was gone, Amber turned to Kelly.

'What is it you don't get about Lockie and Réiltín?'

'Réiltín,' said Kelly. She turned away, took a long drink, spilling some down her chin, then wiping it away with her sleeve. 'The two of them, all in each other's faces. Ew.'

'Leave them alone,' said Amber. 'They're celebrating.'

'Celebrating what?' said Kelly.

'Did LB not tell you?' said Amber. 'Réiltín was his sneaky tutor the whole time – it's how he passed.'

Kelly's eyes shot wide open. 'What?' She turned to LB. 'Why didn't you tell me? When did you find out?'

'Who cares?' said Amber. 'Look, Réiltín seems like a nice person. And it doesn't matter what you think about her.'

'You're my friends!' said Kelly. She looked around at LB for support, but LB's eyes were on the bonfire.

'You're supposed to be on my side!' said Kelly.

'There's only one side!' said Amber. 'What has Réiltín ever done to you?' She stared at Kelly.

Kelly stared back.

'And,' said Amber, 'does *she* have a name for *you* that she accidentally lets slip when you're walking past?'

'You say "Twinkle, twinkle, little freak" too!' said Kelly.

'No, we don't,' said LB, briefly glancing back.

'We were just stupid enough not to stop you doing it,' said Amber.

'Oh, get lost, Amber,' said Kelly.

LB's head spun around. 'Don't tell Amber to get lost!'

'Yeah – grow up,' said Amber.

'She's a psycho!' said Kelly, suddenly. 'Réiltín! She's a psycho!'

LB turned around and shook her head slowly. 'Seriously . . .'

'She is!' said Kelly. She paused.

'Are you trying to make something up?' said Amber.

Kelly glared at her. 'Oh my God – no! She's doing all this on purpose. Being nice to you, the whole thing with Lockie, everything. She's trying to make me jealous. She knows Lockie and I were a thing.'

'Now you're a thing,' said LB.

'That ended last year,' said Amber.

'So?' said Kelly.

'You treated him like crap!' said LB suddenly, her head whipping around to Kelly. 'Like absolute crap!'

Kelly's mouth dropped open. 'What the . . . no, I didn't. How can you even say that?'

'Because it's the truth!' said LB.

Amber nodded.

'If I treated him so badly,' said Kelly, glaring at them, 'why is he still friends with me?'

'What's Lockie going to do?' said LB. 'Not be friends with you, and we all still are, and—'

'What do you mean?' said Kelly. 'Are you saying he's only pretending to be friends with me?'

'No!' said LB. 'That's not what I meant—'

'Because I can go over right now and ask him,' said Kelly, stabbing her can towards him.

'Oh my God,' said LB, 'what I was saying was—'

'I get it,' said Kelly. 'I'm a horrible human being, I treat everyone badly, none of you want me around. Everyone hates me. Fine. I get it.'

'What?' said LB. 'I didn't say any of that. All I said was—'

'It's fine,' said Kelly. 'Seriously. I get it, OK?' She buried her hands in her hoodie. 'Look, I'm just going to go back to my room. Pack, whatever.'

'Don't,' said LB. 'Stay. Come on. It's our last night. Stay

for the ritual! We can release all this –' she shrugged – 'this whatever.'

'"Negative energy"?' said Kelly. She used air quotes.

Amber pretended not to notice. 'Actually,' she said to LB, 'I need to go back to my room and get my things.'

'For the ritual?' said Kelly. She laughed. 'There's no way you're going to end up doing that. You'll get drunk and end up at the bonfire with some guitar-playing hippie.'

'No, I won't,' said Amber. 'I'm—'

'STOP IT!' said LB, turning to Kelly. 'STOP! Stop telling people how they're going to fail.'

Kelly went very still, eyes wide. In her peripheral vision Amber, breath held, could see Rupert approaching. He was raising handfuls of drinks in plastic cups, looking like he was about to make an announcement. Amber turned to him and gave him a look that settled him in beside her.

'Making popcorn in my head,' he whispered.

In front of them, Kelly and LB stood facing each other – LB incandescent, Kelly horrified.

'Excuse me?' said Kelly, glaring at LB.

'I said stop,' said LB, 'pointing out everything everyone's doing wrong! Not even *doing* wrong – stop pointing out things you *think* are wrong, which are really just things that you don't like. *I don't like it, therefore it's*

227

wrong. I don't like that person, therefore you shouldn't like them either. And if I do? Then there's something wrong with me too. Wrong. Wrong. Wrong. Wrong. Wrong.'

Kelly stared at her. 'Wow.'

'That's what you do!' said LB.

'I have never,' said Kelly, 'ever said you were wrong. Give me one example.'

LB blinked. 'It's not . . .' She let out a frustrated breath. 'That's not the point. I mean . . .'

'It is the point if you're going to accuse me of stuff I didn't do,' said Kelly. 'I'm just standing here, and you're saying horrible things about me. And I'm not even doing anything.'

'You were going on and on about Lockie and Réiltín!' said LB. 'Two people you treat like crap. Maybe that's what they're over there talking about. Is that what you're worried about?'

'You were giving out about Rupert and Amber the other day!' said Kelly.

LB's eyes widened. Amber turned to her. 'What were you saying about me and Rupert?' Her tone was one of mild curiosity.

Kelly frowned. 'She was saying that you exclude everyone with your little weirdnesses—'

'OH MY GOD!' said LB. 'I so did not say that.' She turned

228

to Amber. 'I did not say that. I swear to God. I said—'

'Go on,' said Kelly. 'I want to hear this. Because I know what you said.'

'I said . . .' LB paused. 'I said . . .' She paused again. 'I can't remember what I said exactly, but it was definitely not that. I was saying that . . . maybe what I was saying was that sometimes you guys are talking about things and you're so, like, close that I don't know . . . that I feel like . . . maybe . . . I don't even know what I was saying! But it wasn't bad. And I didn't say "little weirdnesses".'

'Yeah, but it's what you meant,' said Kelly.

'It's not what I meant!' said LB, stamping the ground, splashing her drink up over her cup.

'Wow,' said Kelly. 'Calm down.'

LB's eyes were lit with anger.

Lockie suddenly appeared in the space between Kelly and LB and stopped, glancing down at LB. 'Whoa! What's going on here?'

'Good question!' said Kelly.

'Good question?' said LB. 'Oh my God! I can't— I can't even—' She raised her hands in surrender.

'What have I walked into?' said Lockie.

Rupert and Amber both made *you-don't-want-to-know* faces.

'Gentle people! I'm looking for Réiltín!' Johnny's voice

boomed from behind Lockie. 'How is the no alcohol going down?'

Everyone turned to Kelly.

'Go,' hissed Lockie, angling his body to hide her from view.

LB drained the rest of her drink. Amber poured hers onto the sand and stood on top of the stain. Kelly flipped up her hood and, as she passed Rupert, took the four plastic cups he held out to her. Then she ran away like she was in an egg and spoon race.

39

Johnny stood with Réiltín on the beach, looking around at the crowd.

'Reasonably well behaved. Would you agree?'

Réiltín nodded. 'Absolutely.'

'But the night is middle-aged,' said Johnny. 'That's when the crises happen. Ask Suze.'

Réiltín laughed. 'I think it's going to be fine.'

'Really? Can I place my fortune on that? Can I go home and sleep this off?'

Réiltín looked around, fear flickering in her eyes. Johnny laughed. 'Don't worry, the responsibility is all mine. In my experience, it's all fun and games and nobody loses anything.' He looked at his watch, and then at Réiltín.

'Is there something else?' she said.

'I was just wondering,' said Johnny – 'have you checked on our prisoner?'

Amber and LB were sitting by the bonfire using their hoodies as cushions. A guy with dreadlocks and a guitar sat down beside Amber, and she and LB looked at each other and burst out laughing.

Amber turned to the guitar guy. 'Sorry – it's not you.' She turned back to LB. '*Or maybe it is,*' she mouthed.

LB laughed.

'I wouldn't go there even if I wanted to,' said Amber. 'Just to spite her,' and she made a *Yikes!* face. 'Is that terrible?'

'No,' said LB. 'No, it's not.'

Amber looked around the beach. 'Oh God. Look at Rupert.'

'Oh no,' said LB. 'He's like a lost dog.'

'A giant, beautiful red setter,' said Amber.

'I swear to God . . .' said LB.

'If that guy breaks his heart—' they both said at the same time.

'He won't,' said Amber.

'No,' said LB. 'No way.'

'We would hunt him down and kill him,' said Amber.

Kelly walked across the sand, knocking back vodka, scanning the party with angry eyes. *Réiltín, Réiltín, Réiltín. What the hell is wrong with everyone?* She spotted Rupert

232

wandering around, and was about to head towards him, when she saw Amber and LB sitting at the bonfire. Beside a hippie tuning his guitar.

'Told ya,' said Kelly, leaning between the two of them. She turned to the guy. 'Hello, hippie guitar man. Have you met my friend, Amber?'

Amber turned to him and gave him an apologetic smile. 'I'm so sorry.' She used LB's shoulder to push herself up onto her feet, and turned to Kelly.

'Well, that was rude,' said Amber.

'No, it wasn't,' said Kelly. 'It was funny.'

'We weren't even talking to the poor guy,' said Amber.

'So, we don't even know him, so it doesn't matter,' said Kelly. She shrugged, and leaned out. 'Sorry, hippie guitar man, for any offence I may have caused. Or not, probably.'

Amber stared at her.

'What is wrong with you guys tonight?' said Kelly.

'Oh my God,' said Amber. 'There's nothing wrong with us. It's you!'

LB jumped up from the sand and moved in beside Amber.

'Fine, I get it,' said Kelly. 'Réiltín is amazing, Lockie's amazing, you're all amazing, and I'm a bitch.'

'No,' said Amber, 'no one has said any of those things. It's literally like Kelly Translate! You put the words in and whatever comes out is a foreign language. Or just lies.'

'I'm not lying,' said Kelly.

'Distorting the truth?' said Amber.

Kelly swayed in front of her.

'Can you actually listen to what people are saying?' said Amber. 'It's in English. And try not to process it through your messed-up translation software. Listen to the words I'm saying. But don't expect me to respond to the words you're hearing.'

Kelly snorted. 'Why are you *so* angry?'

Amber let out a breath. She looked around at people smiling and laughing. Behind them, the guy with the guitar started to play. 'It's our last night,' said Amber. 'We shouldn't be fighting—'

'I wasn't the one fighting!' shouted Kelly. 'You were the ones—'

'Oh, just shut up, Kelly! Shut up!' said LB. 'Just shut up when someone's trying to apologise—'

'Whoa,' said Amber. 'I was not trying to apologise.'

'I meant you were trying to calm things down,' said LB.

'Oh my God,' said Kelly, 'when you were the ones losing it!'

Amber and LB exchanged glances.

'I can't,' said Amber, shaking her head. 'I can't.'

'Do you know what?' said Kelly. 'Just go off, the two of you . . .' She looked at Amber. 'Go off, grab your crystals

234

and your little tiny moon, and do your stupid—'

'Things are not stupid,' said Amber, 'just because you don't like them! Or get them! Or . . . or because they make you feel like you're not the centre of the universe!'

'Wow,' said Kelly.

'Wow,' said Amber, imitating her. She turned to LB. 'Have you ever noticed? Kelly says "wow" every time someone tells a truth about her that she doesn't like. If they get angry enough, they'll say it, but Kelly just gets to say "wow", which is her smoke bomb. "Look over there at *her* anger! Don't look at me and the truth she just told about me."' Amber turned and walked away. 'I'm not waiting for your "wow" this time,' she called back.

Kelly could feel LB's eyes on her, but stood, steely-eyed, staring ahead, until LB slipped from her side and ran across the beach after Amber.

Kelly stayed where she was, arms crossed, looking for something or someone or anything. She saw Rupert, head high, scanning the beach. She ran towards him.

'So Amber just went nuts,' said Kelly.

'Amber?' said Rupert.

'I know,' said Kelly. 'She said all these horrible things.'

'Amber?' said Rupert. 'Sorry – no.'

'She did. It was insane. And LB ran after her. Like, Amber stormed off.'

'Why did she storm off?' said Rupert. 'Is she OK?'

'I don't know,' said Kelly. 'Relax. She's fine. LB ran after her.'

Rupert didn't respond.

Kelly turned to him so suddenly he flinched. She laughed. 'Walk me back to my room, Rupe? I'm done.'

'What?' said Rupert. 'No. I'm meeting Tadhg.'

'*Ohhh*,' said Kelly. 'Exciting.'

Rupert looked around, nervous.

'Oh no – is he late? Do you think he's not coming? OK, if he doesn't show—'

'Of course he's going to show!' said Rupert. 'He's the one who asked me—'

'Mmm, OK, but if he doesn't, you can come to my room. We'll have drinks, yeah?'

Rupert turned to her. 'He's coming, Kelly. OK?'

'No, I know,' said Kelly. 'I know.' She started walking backwards. 'I'm going to go now. I can walk back myself. Don't forget, though . . . But he'll come! I know he will! Like – look at you! *Gorgeous!*'

She took a few more steps backwards, then pirouetted around, tossed her hair, threw her arms up high, and walked away on tiptoes across the sand.

You little scorpion, thought Rupert. *Always a sting in the tail.*

40

Réiltín and Lockie stood in a quiet spot on the beach.

'Listen, thanks again,' said Lockie. 'Not just for Irish, but for listening . . . about Clare.'

'I don't know if I really did anything,' said Réiltín. 'Especially since you just saved my life.'

He laughed.

'Seriously, I owe you, though,' said Réiltín. 'I might not have died, but I could have got an elbow in the face.'

'You did really help, Réiltín. You listened to me. I mean, I can talk to LB, and Rupe's great. But I'm just so used to talking to Clare about everything. Like, stuff I couldn't say to the others. So it's weird not having her. Suddenly, she's just gone.'

'Only temporarily,' said Réiltín.

'Do you really think that?' said Lockie.

'Yes!' said Réiltín. She pulled out her phone and handed

it to him. 'Call her, see.' She smiled.

'I can't. No way. Her dad!'

'He can't answer her phone,' said Réiltín.

Lockie raised his eyebrows. 'Oh yes he can.'

'Well, then – he'll get me,' said Réiltín. 'Punch in the number.'

Lockie did as she said, and handed her back the phone when it started to ring. Réiltín put it up to her ear, and smiled and nodded when the call was picked up.

'Hi. Is this Clare?'

'No. This is Clare's father.'

Réiltín panicked and put the phone on speaker so Lockie could hear.

'Is this you again?' said Clare's father. 'Have you a new phone to harass my daughter on? I can tell you now, if you call, or text, or message, or come within an inch of my daughter, I'll be going to the police about this . . .'

Lockie looked at Réiltín, alarmed.

'. . . and I have Clare's permission to do so.'

Lockie opened his mouth to speak, but Réiltín shook her head, took the phone off speaker, and put it up to her ear.

'I'm sorry, sir. This is a misunderstanding. My name is—' She listened to him, frowning. 'No,' she said, 'my name is Réiltín Raye. I don't know anything about any of that.' She listened again, then, shaking her head, said,

238

'I'm being called away now. I have to go. Sorry.' She ended the call.

'What the hell?' said Lockie. 'Clare gave her dad permission to go to the police? About what? Why? Could you hear her, in the background or anything?'

Réiltín shook her head.

'What an asshole,' said Lockie. He turned to Réiltín. 'Sorry. It's just . . . what the hell's happening?' He stood with his hands on his head, looking around, his eyes filled with panic.

'I'm so sorry,' said Réiltín. She checked her phone. 'And now I have to go back to the rooms. Are you OK? I could get the others—'

'No – go,' said Lockie. 'You're on duty. I'm fine. Seriously.'

'Are you sure?' said Réiltín.

Lockie nodded. 'Seriously. Go.'

Réiltín gave him a small smile, and tucked her phone into her back pocket. 'I'll be back. Go to the bonfire. Don't be on your own.'

Lockie nodded. 'Thanks.'

He watched her jog away, then sat down and stared out at the sea. What was happening? His chest swelled with a familiar sensation that tightened his throat and made his heart pound and sucked him back to his mother's funeral, standing by her graveside, watching the coffin straps slide through the funeral directors' hands as they lowered the coffin into the ground, but then the worst ever – the hands he watched scoop up a fist of dirt from the mound beside the grave and throw in on top of her, because he couldn't understand why. Why would anyone do that? And hating them for doing it. And it didn't matter that his dad had explained to him it was about returning her body to the earth, because why did the earth get to have her when *he* wanted her? Why was she going down into the dark when she was the furthest thing from the dark he had ever known?

Lockie's chest heaved. He sucked in breath after breath, struggling to force down the thought that came next: *Until Clare*. A rush of emptiness swept through him and his heart felt cracked open. He bowed his head, and saw something gleam in his peripheral vision. He turned towards it. His eyes locked onto a glass bottle half-wedged in the sand, a curve of amber liquid visible. He glanced around, but there was no one nearby. He walked over, pulled it out, and held it up to the light.

Hello, whiskey. Yes, I'll be dying tomorrow. But let's just live for tonight.

41

Rupert sat on a rock by the shoreline, hypnotised by the swish and roll of the waves. He let out a long breath, then spoke to himself out loud: '"Everything is imaginable," Rupert lied.' Because he couldn't imagine never seeing Tadhg again – someone he didn't even know the day he had first spoken those words and meant them. *Three weeks ago.* Rupert couldn't even imagine not seeing Tadhg at breakfast, or leaving and not getting to say goodbye. His next breath was a gentle sigh. Because he could still imagine their wedding photos.

'You were not joking.' The voice came from behind him. Rupert's heart jumped. He turned to see Tadhg standing before him, fresh from the shower, gleaming and beaming in a white T-shirt and blue jeans.

'I was not joking,' said Rupert, standing up, gesturing to his white shorts and his black-and-white striped top.

'The light,' said Rupert, 'is on the inside.'

'I see it,' said Tadhg.

Amber sat on the sand, hood up, knees to her chest, with the rest of the hoodie engulfing her down to her ankles, her feet peeping out.

'This party,' said LB, 'is officially alcohol-free.'

'Yet still she skips,' said Amber.

'Not even soft drinks,' said LB. 'Food truck is closed.' She sat down beside Amber, copied her hoodie arrangement.

'We drank way too quickly,' said Amber.

'I always drink way more when Kelly's around,' said LB. 'Or I feel like I need to be sober to look after her. And—'

'You know you're not her minder,' said Amber.

LB laughed. 'She's *my* minder.'

'You don't need a minder,' said Amber.

'I so do,' said LB. 'The amount of times she's come to my rescue when people come up all, "Are you Antsy's daughter?" or they're trying to take sneaky photos. Especially if I'm up to no good.'

Amber laughed. 'You're never up to no good.'

'Apart from the breaking into places and stealing?' said LB. 'This place has changed me.' She laughed.

'Did you put Johnny's building plan back?'

LB nodded. 'When I went down to make the call.'

Rupert's glorious laughter floated up into the night, and they looked over to where he stood beaming at a shy-looking Tadhg, who was standing with one hand in his pocket, the other twirling his car keys.

LB and Amber exchanged glances.

'It's going to be me again, isn't it?' said LB.

'Not so fast,' said Amber. 'I think you've served your time.'

Amber, head light, limbs loose, squinted as she ran through the bright white perimeter lights that shone through the trees bordering the college drive. The strobe effect was starting to tug at her stomach, so to keep herself steady she focused her gaze on Rupert, six feet in front. Tadhg was up ahead, on a sober sprint. Amber slowed to a stop, clutching her stomach. Rupert glanced around and jogged back when he saw her.

'Are you OK?' he said.

Amber nodded, letting out a long breath. 'I'm fine.' She reached out and squeezed his arm, smiled up at his concerned face. 'But I can't believe you've made me come too. The whole point is you getting to have a romantic drive with Tadhg. The alcohol run was just an excuse. You two could be alone!'

'Exactly!' hissed Rupert.

42

Lockie stood with his back to the closed food truck. He leaned out and squinted into the low light. Something looked like it was floating in front of gold ribbons hovering over two lollipop sticks. He blinked and saw the college hoodie, and legs and, for a moment, a flash of skin from inside the hood.

'Stop looking around for someone to rescue you!' snapped Johnny.

Lockie jerked back in, pressing himself against the side of the truck, squeezing his eyes shut.

No drinking. Stay out of trouble. Stay away from girls.

'Grow up!' shouted Johnny. 'Have you not got it yet? No one is coming to rescue you. No one even knows you're here!'

Lockie felt a stab of sobriety shoot through him. Was that Kelly? What was Johnny going to do?

No drinking. Stay out of trouble. Stay away from girls.

Lockie straightened his shoulders. *Screw this.* He started to step out from the side of the truck.

'Réiltín!' he heard Johnny roar. 'Réiltín!'

Lockie pressed back into the truck. He could hear footsteps on the sand.

'Will you take her back to the Lodge?' said Johnny.

'Sure,' said Réiltín.

Lockie froze, staggered backwards and away.

Rupert sat in the car, back straight, hands on his knees, staring out through the windscreen, his heart rate intermittently spiking, as Tadhg drove the winding, pitch-black roads. He glanced down at Tadhg's hand as he shifted gears effortlessly, taking the car quickly and smoothly around every bend without going over the speed limit.

'The speed limit on country roads is insane,' said Amber, bouncing on the back seat.

'That's what the "Oh Jesus!" handle is for,' said Tadhg.

Amber looked at him blankly.

'Above the window,' said Tadhg.

Amber smiled. 'Thank you.' She looked at Rupert. 'You're very relaxed.'

Rupert nodded. 'I'm used to country roads,' he said.

And there are other things to be not relaxed about. Has anyone done a survey on the anticipation and associated terror of a first kiss? Is there any difference between a first kiss – heterosexual, and a first kiss – gay? And a first kiss – bi, when you've already kissed the opposite sex? What about a first kiss with someone you've just met, and a first kiss with someone you've fallen immediately in love with? A first kiss that was unexpected versus a first kiss that you've been imagining for weeks? A first kiss you've imagined one way – in an empty dining room, say, over a breakfast buffet – but then might happen in an unimaginable way . . . involving GAA. 'Everything is imaginable,' Rupert lied, in this case.

Lockie reached the main part of the beach, scanning it for a familiar face, and instead saw the bright blonde head of LB. She was sitting alone. He flopped down hard beside her.

'What the hell is going on with Kelly?' said Lockie. 'And Johnny?'

'Oh God,' said LB, 'what's she done now?'

'He caught her, drunk. I was about to go get her, but he called Réiltín instead.'

They exchanged glances. 'Réiltín with Drunk Kelly?' said LB.

'Where are Amber and Rupert?' said Lockie.

'Tadhg's driving them to get more drink. To the GAA

246

club, apparently. There's no garage open nearby. He works shifts there, so it's not exactly breaking in . . .'

'Because if it was, you'd be doing it.'

LB laughed.

'Not a risk a celebrity daughter wants to take,' said Lockie.

They looked across the water to Carraig na nGealt. 'Are we really doing this?' said Lockie. 'Climbing that?'

'I want to,' said LB. 'For Amber, more than anything. She was having such a hard time before she came here. And I think being here with everyone, being away, has kind of . . . I don't know . . . lightened her up? This really means something to her. But I think it's more than that. She's very intuitive . . . I think she's doing it to try to . . . well, bring us together again.'

'It didn't work out for all the king's horses and all the king's men,' said Lockie.

LB laughed again. 'That was "couldn't put Humpty together again", though.'

'Oh yeah,' said Lockie.

'And we aren't broken,' said LB.

Lockie nodded. 'And we haven't had a great fall.'

Amber sat in the back seat of the car, her free hand in her trouser pocket, hot fingers clutching the small Rock

Paper Scissors deck. It was just backup. In case not doing a reading for over twenty-four hours would make her so anxious that she wouldn't enjoy the night. She felt a little stab of guilt. She'd promised Rupert. But, still – it wasn't like she was going to do something that would hurt her, was it? . . . But she knew it wasn't about the sneaky deck. It was about lying to Rupe. And breaking promises.

Tadhg slowed the car, and parked by the side of the road.

'Sorry, lads!' he said, unhooking his seatbelt. 'Comfort break.' He hopped out. Then he poked his head back in the door. 'If any of the rest of you need to . . . use the facilities . . .'

'No, thank you,' said Amber as he disappeared.

Rupert spun around to her. 'Etiquette nightmare. I *do* need comfort. But, like, where? Do I follow him? Will he think I'm a weirdo? Or will he think I'm weird if I go in the opposite direction? Do I wait—'

'He's gone that way,' said Amber, pointing ahead. 'You go that way.' She gestured with her thumb out of the back window.

'This is exhausting,' said Rupert, undoing his seat belt.

As soon as the door closed, Amber took the deck out of her pocket, opened it, and slid out the cards. She closed her eyes, and said, "Tell me something about tonight."' She shuffled and two cards flew out. One landed on Rupert's seat, face down. She grabbed it quickly, flipped it over. SCISSORS, with the word ENDINGS. The line underneath said *Cut Out All That No Longer Serves You.*

She nodded. That made sense. That's what full-moon rituals were all about. She leaned in between the front seats to see if the second card had landed in one of the passenger footwells, then jumped back as Tadhg yanked open the driver's door and sat back in.

Kelly lay on her bed, head swimming. *What was wrong with everyone? It was their last night. It was supposed to be fun. And she was stuck in. Why? Because of a stupid rule. And a stupid bitch was supposed to be checking on her?* She slammed her head back onto the pillow, slammed her fists down. It was like when she was a kid in the summer with her early bedtime when the sun was still bright and she could hear all the other kids playing outside. Tears sprung into her eyes . . .

Why are Amber and LB being bitches? After everything I did for them, they do this? And Lockie and Réiltín? What the hell? Oh my God – if they end up doing that stupid ritual, and she ends up going to that, and I'm the one not there— Réiltín probably planned this as soon as she knew we were coming. That's what psychos do. Tear things apart and tell people they're fixing them. Oh my God – Réiltín was trying to make it like all their problems would be solved as long as she was out of the way. Bye bye, Kelly. Hello, Little Freak . . .

Kelly sprung up in the bed. No one knew what a psycho Réiltín was. And they were probably going to invite her to the ritual, and even though she was rules, rules, rules, she'd go. They were the best friends in the world – why wouldn't she want to steal them from her? Kelly cried harder. They really were the best friends in the world and now she was fighting with them.

Kelly jumped out of bed, grabbed her hoodie and pulled it on, slipped into her Vans. She looked around, made some rearrangements to the room, and headed for the door.

Full-moon ritual. Forgiveness and letting go, right?

I release Réiltín.

She smiled.

And grant myself forgiveness.

43

Réiltín settled Suze into Room 5 and closed the door gently behind her.

She felt bad for Suze, and bad for Johnny. But as she turned right to go down to Kelly's room, she felt a sudden thrill. She felt like herself, which was weird, because this wasn't herself – drinking, and hanging out with Lockie Loughnane. Being *friends* with Lockie Loughnane. Her heart flipped at the thought of walking around with Lockie in school, everyone seeing him laughing the way he always laughed at her jokes. And there was LB too. And she got on well with Rupert and Amber. If Rupert and Tadhg ended up together, then there was no way she wouldn't end up hanging out with them. They were actually a really nice group of friends. Couldn't they *see* Kelly?

In the back seat of Tadhg's car, Amber's heel was on the second oracle card that had slid, face down, under Rupert's seat. She was trying to slide it towards her so she could pick it up. The car bounced and her heel lifted.

'Here we are now,' said Tadhg, gesturing to the sign for the GAA club, slowing the car, indicating right, then pulling into the ditch to park.

Amber unhooked her seat belt.

'Are you coming in with us?' said Tadhg.

'Oh, no,' said Amber. 'I just wanted to stretch.' She bent down and picked up the card, slid it onto her thigh, face down with her hand covering it.

'Oh. No one's going anywhere,' said Tadhg, pointing to the entrance gate to the club, blocked by a van that was parked in front of it.

'The End!' said Rupert.

'Let me go and check if there's anyone in it,' said Tadhg. He opened the car door and the light came on. Amber flipped the oracle card over, and glanced down. Her stomach tightened. 'Oh my God,' she said.

'Oh your God what?' said Rupert.

Amber hesitated. 'Just, oh my God – we can't get in.'

Tadhg jumped back into the car. 'Nope. That's one empty van.'

Amber leaned forward. 'Maybe you could hop in over

the gate? Just park further up?'

'I could,' said Tadhg. 'But that would take way longer.'

Everyone looked at the blue glow of 22:05 on the clock.

'We need to get back,' said Rupert.

'Is there anywhere else we could go?' said Amber.

'Nowhere's open,' said Tadhg.

'Are we that desperate for alcohol?' said Rupert. 'Said Rupert in judgement.'

'Don't ask me! I'm just the getaway driver,' said Tadhg.

'And the get-there driver. And the thwarted thief.'

'I'd like to make it very clear,' said Tadhg, 'that I intended to leave cash.'

'None of that is the point,' said Rupert. 'We need to get back for the ritual. Everyone will be waiting. We have bad habits to get rid of. Out with the old!'

'What ritual?' said Tadhg.

He was about to turn around to Amber when she slid forward in her seat. 'Guys, I'm not . . . feeling well.'

She scrambled from the car.

Kelly stood at the arched window in the attic room, watching the full moon over Carraig na nGealt. Her finger was holding open a notebook on a page titled *How to do a full-moon ritual*, with a bullet-pointed list underneath, all in Amber's handwriting. Amber would have to be back for her stuff. Kelly could wait for her. She picked up the selenite sphere on the stand, rubbed it in her hands, and put it back down again. She examined each of the crystals around it.

On the bed beside her, Amber's green rucksack was open. Kelly opened it wider, and rooted inside. Candles – check. Sage smudge stick – check. Amber's treasure chest – check. Clicky lighter – check. Other random crystals, an incense burner, whatever, but – check. 'Everything you could possibly need – except me!' She made a sad face. *Me being there is probably what you don't need*. She sat on the bed, her hand resting on the open bag, then she walked her fingers back over to the treasure chest, and took it out. She opened it, saw some pens, some blank pages, and some with handwriting on them.

'Stop,' she said, flipping it closed, pushing it back into the bag. She looked at the alarm clock and the flashing 22:30. Why hadn't Amber come for her stuff? Maybe she was drunk with some hippie. Or maybe she was just running late. Kelly stood up, packed the bag, carefully wrapped up the selenite sphere, put that in on top, then zipped up the whole thing and left it on the bed.

She paused at the top of the stairs and looked around. No crystals, no candles, no incense, no decks. No Amberness. She made another sad face. She really loved Amberness.

Rupert had his back against the passenger door of the car, arms crossed, legs crossed. Tadhg was standing in front of him, thumbs hooked into his back pockets, looking up at the sky, around at the trees, back up at the sky.

'The moon,' said Tadhg.

'I know,' said Rupert.

'It's so *bright*,' said Tadhg.

Rupert nodded, feeling the more at ease of the two of them, until the sharp, alarming shift in his chest as Tadhg finally lowered his gaze to him.

'Too bright,' Rupert blurted.

Tadhg laughed. 'All the better to see you with.'

The Big Gay Wolf. Rupert's heart pounded. He would be eaten alive. They locked eyes. There was a fractional lean-in. From the darkness behind them came the sound of Amber puking.

'That cannot be our soundtrack,' said Rupert.

Réiltín drew back into the corridor from Kelly and LB's room and quietly closed the door. Prisoner present and accounted for. Her phone started to ring, and she jumped to answer it.

'Tadhg? What's going on? LB told me you went out to get drinks. Where are you?'

'On the side of the road, on the way back from the club,'

said Tadhg. 'Amber's . . . not well.' He lowered his voice. 'I can't risk her puking in the back of my car. So we'll probably be a little while.'

'Oh God,' said Réiltín. 'This night . . . What's "a little while"? I'm supposed to be signing people in for the night. I know it's the last night. And I wasn't going to be super strict, but still . . .'

'I don't know – a quarter of an hour?' said Tadhg.

'Oh, OK. That's not too bad.'

'Hold on,' said Tadhg, 'Rupert's shouting at me. About some ritual Amber was doing . . . Tell the others it's off.'

'What ritual?' said Réiltín.

Rupert took the phone from Tadhg. 'Hi Réiltín. Nothing major. We were just going do a full-moon ritual. Amber was doing it, and now she can't, obviously. It was meant to be at ten thirty. Could you let the others know? Just in case they're waiting?'

'Waiting where?' said Réiltín. 'Where were you doing it?'

Rupert hesitated. 'On . . . on the beach.'

'Where on the beach? So I can find them.' said Réiltín.

'Um . . . the dunes?' said Rupert. 'At the end?'

'OK,' said Réiltín. 'Can you put Tadhg back on?'

'Hi,' said Tadhg. 'Just one more job for Rézer.'

'And the irony is the one person I don't have to worry

about is Kelly Warner. She's actually where she's supposed to be. Incarcerated.'

Kelly, hovering behind a crack in the door to 3A, smiled. *Yeah. LB's army bag is fast asleep.* When Réiltín was gone, Kelly sprinted back up the stairs and grabbed Amber's backpack. The least she could do to make it up to her was to have everything ready to . . . *rock*! She smiled. 'It has steps!' LB had said. 'You can walk across to it in five minutes! Get to the top in fifteen!' Kelly shrugged. *How hard can it be?*

44

Lockie and LB were sitting on the dunes, looking out over Carraig na nGealt. LB turned to see Kelly weaving her way towards them. She seemed to be wearing a backpack, as she was holding onto the straps.

'Oh God,' said LB, standing up. 'What's she doing out again?'

'Act normal,' said Lockie. 'Please. I don't want to get into anything tonight. Or any night.'

'Hey!' said LB as Kelly reached them and stopped to heave for breath.

Kelly pointed to Carraig na nGealt.

'OK, here's the deal . . .' She glanced behind her. 'Checking for Réiltín . . .'

'I thought she was putting you to bed,' said Lockie.

'What?' said Kelly. 'Nobody put me to bed. I wasn't *that* bad. She was *checking* on me in bed. But I put LB's bag in it. I knew Réiltín wasn't going to come right up to me.' She glanced over her shoulder again. 'So, Amber and the others are on the way, running late, so let's just go ahead.'

'Why don't we just wait?' said Lockie.

'No,' said Kelly, shaking her head. 'If we set everything up—'

'Is that all her stuff?' said LB, pointing to the backpack. 'She'll go nuts.'

'No, she won't,' said Kelly. 'It was all just out there in her room. Nothing we hadn't seen before. I just put it in a bag.' She paused. 'I forgot to leave her a note.'

Lockie and LB exchanged glances.

Kelly nodded. 'Yeah – she'll know it was me.'

Amber drifted awake on the back seat of the car. She slowly sat up, and blinked. She was alone. She looked out of the window. She could see the dunes up ahead, and she knew she was right by the causeway to Carraig na nGealt. Where were Rupert and Tadhg? She looked right and could see Tadhg jogging away in the direction of the Lodge, pushing his phone into his back pocket. Where was Rupe?

Amber opened the door, got out, and could see Rupert and Kelly standing on the dune, briefly hugging before Kelly disappeared down the other side.

Amber walked over, yawning, and called up to Rupert. 'Why are we here? What's Kelly doing?' Rupert reached out a hand for Amber to come up to him.

When she got to the top, she looked down and saw the others.

'I've got all your stuff!' said Kelly.

'What stuff?' said Amber.

'For the full-moon ritual,' said Kelly.

Amber looked up at Rupert. 'But we called it off—'

'Get your asses moving!' said Kelly.

Amber's eyes shot wide. 'What? No – we're not doing this. Seriously. We called it off.'

'When?' said LB.

'On the phone to Réiltín,' said Rupert.

LB looked at Kelly, who was looking away.

'Asses!' said Kelly. 'I'm telling you – Réiltín's on the way!'

'We're back now,' said Rupert to Amber. 'You look a bit brighter.' He paused. 'Or would you prefer to go back to your room?'

Amber looked around at everyone. 'Are you all going up?' They nodded.

'But seriously,' said Kelly, 'Réiltín really is on her way.'

'I don't think I feel up to it,' said Amber.

'I'll do it if you don't want to,' said Kelly, holding the straps of the bag tight.

'You can't do that,' said LB. 'This is Amber's night.'

'It's not my night—'

'It's all our nights,' said Kelly over her.

Amber looked up at Rupert. 'Can I borrow you please? I need to get something out of the car.'

'Sure,' said Rupert.

Amber pulled him out of sight of the others, behind the dunes.

'No, no, no,' said Amber, voice low, eyes wide. 'We can't do this.' She was bouncing on her toes, shaking out her hands.

'It's OK,' said Rupert. 'We don't have to go. I'm not going to go without you, obviously—'

'But all the others are going to go,' said Amber.

'Not without you, either.'

She shook her head. 'Kelly will persuade them. I can't exactly tell her not to.' She looked around. 'Is Tadhg coming back?'

'No,' said Rupert. 'He's not going to crash a friends thing. Besides, releasing a fear of kissing boys and liking it is something one should do in *private*.'

Amber smiled, but then she slowly raised a trembling hand. 'OK, well that's another reason not to do it,' she said.

'Hey,' Rupert said, gently holding her forearms. 'What's up?'

'I've got a really bad feeling.'

He nodded. 'Because you were ill.'

Amber shook her head. 'I'm not, Rupe. I'm so sorry . . . I was faking. I . . . I stuck my fingers down my throat. I know – don't say anything. I know . . . I'm sorry.'

'But . . . why?' said Rupert.

'I'm so embarrassed. About all of it.' Tears welled in Amber's eyes. 'Because of this.' She reached into her back pocket and pulled out the small black-and-red Rock Paper Scissors oracle card and handed it to him. It said: DANGER! ROCKFALLS. The picture at the centre was a triangle warning sign with a rock, and loose rocks falling from it, and, underneath it, *Serious Risk of Injury or Death*. The line at the bottom was *Lies Are Like Loose Rocks*.

Rupert looked up at her. 'Is this the sinister deck? Rupert did not need to ask.'

Amber laughed, and tears spilled down her cheeks.

'Literally who,' said Rupert, 'would want to know something like this? And also, I'm presuming the message from these cards is not so much about the picture, but about the line at the bottom? That lies are dangerous, and when they're "dislodged", like falling rocks, they can hurt people.' He paused. 'But only if the people are at the bottom. So . . . "rise above the lies" – that's the message. Or hold tight to them, so they don't get loose in the first place.'

'I know I shouldn't be paying attention to an oracle card, or making decisions based on what it says,' said Amber.

'That's all I need to hear,' said Rupert.

Amber smiled.

Rupert took her hand, and turned back towards the others. Behind him, she glanced up at Carraig na nGealt. Dark clouds drifted across the moon, and a look of dread across Amber's face.

LB had arranged it so that Lockie was standing in between her and Kelly. Kelly was bouncing on her feet, impatient, when Amber and Rupert appeared on top of the dune. Rupert raised Amber's hand.

Amber looked at the others. 'Are you all, maybe, not sober enough to be doing this?'

Rupert looked at her. 'I don't think the lunatics were one hundred per cent, either.'

Réiltín jogged down the beach. In the distance, she could see from the mop of hair, and the height difference, two figures she thought must be Rupert and Amber, standing on the dunes. They were back. Réiltín slowed to a stop. Then their ritual was back on, whatever it was. She didn't want to act like a loser and crash that on their last night . . . Rupert and Amber disappeared down the other side of the dunes. Réiltín paused. But, then again, she wanted to make sure they weren't back too late, either . . . She headed for the dunes.

When she got to the top, she stood watching the disappearing backs of the five Very Important People she was being paid to supervise. Her heart sank. How could they do this? On the last night? They knew that if they got caught, *she'd* be the one in trouble the most. Then her stomach flipped. *Antsy's daughter in tragic fall* . . . Réiltín stood with her hands on her head, turning towards the Lodge, then back again. Then she ran after the people she thought were friends.

45

Lockie heard his name being called. He glanced back, and saw Réiltín running towards him, waving. He stopped, and ran back to her.

'What the hell?' said Réiltín. 'What are you thinking? Who's gone over?'

'All of us,' said Lockie. 'Sorry, but . . .'

'I can't believe you're doing this,' said Réiltín.

'Not on purpose,' said Lockie. 'I mean – nobody wants to get you in trouble.'

'Ironically,' said Réiltín, 'Kelly's the only one who won't.'

Lockie made an apologetic face. 'Actually . . .'

'What the hell? But . . . I just saw her in bed.'

'Nope,' said Lockie, 'that was LB's bag.'

'Oh my God,' said Réiltín. 'I am so dead. I am *so* dead. I just told Johnny she's on lockdown, and he's gone off to bed. And what the hell? I need to stop you guys. Seriously. This is insane.'

'The only reason we didn't say anything is you were busy. We knew you'd worry . . . It's all going to be wrapped up in an hour, anyway, according to Amber. Like, including getting up and back.'

'That's not the point—'

'But if Johnny's asleep,' said Lockie, 'then it doesn't matter—'

'If Johnny's already asleep, he'll definitely be awake about seven hours from now, which, if you don't stick to your timing, is the earliest you idiots will get back across.'

'What do you mean?' said Lockie.

'Tidal island?' said Réiltín. 'The tide will be in within the hour.'

On top of the rock, under the full moon, Amber and Kelly were at the healing well, setting everything up around it for the ritual. The candles were grouped on the stone ledge above the well, shining in the narrow streams of water that trickled down the rock, glowing against the chipped and faded religious statues and empty candle holders, their red plastic turned a pale shade of coral. On the ground next to the well, on its little stand, was Amber's selenite sphere, glowing like the moon.

LB was sitting on a grassy mound, her eyes on Kelly, her jaw clenched.

Rupert came up beside her. 'Not interested in the set-up?'

LB smiled. 'Not interested in being around Kelly right now.' She looked at him. 'But in the spirit of letting things go . . .'

Kelly laughed over to them, and pointed to herself and Amber, and their hoods. 'We look like monks.'

'Solemnly tending to our religious artefacts,' said Amber.

LB glanced at Rupert. 'How come you're wearing your crime scene?' she said, pointing to his college hoodie.

He leaned down and smelled it. 'Because it's m'boyfriend's. I was a little chilly in the night air. He's never getting it back. Even if I have to lose an arm to the clothes bank to do swapsies.' He smelled it again, offered it to LB. She laughed. 'Laundry. Nice.'

'He smells like life itself,' said Rupert.

LB laughed again. 'How did your drive go?'

'Well, I made the decision not to mention the whole "in love" thing until at least the first kiss.'

'Oh, wow,' said LB. 'The restraint.'

'Just until later, I suspect.' He paused. 'I have this fear of kissing boys I need to let go of.' He smiled. It was nervous.

LB side-eyed him. 'What's that about? Is there reluctance there?'

'No,' said Rupert. 'Not reluctance.' His gaze drifted towards Kelly. LB followed it.

'What?' said LB. 'Something to do with Kelly?'

Rupert looked around, leaned in to LB. 'I don't want to ruin anyone's night . . .'

LB frowned at him. 'But you look so sad.'

Tears welled in Rupert's eyes. 'Oh God . . . sorry.' He turned away from the others.

'It's OK,' said LB. 'It's always OK.'

Rupert let out a shaky sigh, tipped his head back, blinked away his tears. 'He's so sweet – Tadhg. When we were coming back in the car, a text came in from Johnny to say there was a call from Páidí, our neighbour, and I was to call him back. Anyway, I just thought it was about picking me up from the train station, and Tadhg lent me his phone, and anyway . . .' He spoke through fresh tears. 'Dad's been in hospital since last Monday . . . Everything's fine; he's OK; there's a problem with his heart, but he's OK. They didn't want to worry me. And poor Páidí is coming all the way here to pick me up tomorrow . . . He'll take me to Dad on the way home.'

'Oh, sweetheart,' said LB. She gave him a huge hug. 'I'm so sorry. I'm glad he's OK, though. And they were right not to worry you . . . And he'll be so looking forward to seeing you.'

'Me too,' said Rupert, tears spilling down his face. He let out another sigh. 'Right!' he said, pulling down the sleeve of Tadhg's hoodie, wiping his eyes. 'That's when he gave me this. And a little kiss on the cheek.'

Kelly stood up from straightening the candles and turned around to see Lockie walking towards her.

'There he is – slow-moving vehicle,' she said, opening her arms, walking towards him. 'Sweating like a . . .' She stopped when she saw Réiltín following a few feet behind him.

'Oh my *God*!' said Kelly, eyes instantly alight. 'What the hell is *she* doing here?'

'What the hell is wrong with you?' said Lockie, taking Kelly's elbow, and guiding her further away, out of Réiltín's earshot. 'Keep your voice down, will you?'

'Oh my God,' said Kelly again, eyes wild. 'She cannot be here—'

'She *shouldn't* be here because she could get killed—'

'Yeah – by me,' said Kelly.

'Grow up,' said Lockie. 'There's no reason she *can't* be here. *I* said come up, because I knew there'd be a hope of the whole thing wrapping up in time if she was here.' He paused. 'And I like her, OK?'

269

'Who's suddenly on a timer?' said Kelly. She grabbed him by the shirt. 'I'm telling you – go over there and tell her to get her ass back down—'

'We all have to get our asses down,' said Lockie, pulling her hands away. 'This is insane.'

'We haven't even done the ritual yet,' said Kelly. 'What – we climb all the way—'

'Listen to me!' said Lockie.

'. . . up here,' continued Kelly, ignoring him, 'and . . .' She paused, glancing over at Réiltín, then back at Lockie. 'Oh, are we all in trouble now with the *cuinteoir*? Is that why we have to go? We're having fun, so let's end that?'

'No!' hissed Lockie. 'She's trying to look out for us. Would you listen! We have to get down off the rock, *now*, or we'll be cut off by the tide and stuck here for hours.'

'Yeah, right,' said Kelly, looking over towards Réiltín. 'She's totally making that up. Why wouldn't you just have come up here on your own to tell us that? She could have sent you up.'

'What you're not getting,' said Lockie, 'is that, whether you like it or not, she's kind of responsible for us, so she wants to make sure we actually all get off safely—'

'That's ridiculous,' said Kelly. 'What difference can she make? What's she going to do? Break someone's fall? The size of her.'

Lockie put his hands on his hips, shook his head.

Kelly leaned into his face. 'You're so thick. How can you not see what she's doing? She just wants to get into the group. She starts with you – obviously saw you were vulnerable—'

'I wasn't "vulnerable",' said Lockie. 'I was sad, like a normal person.'

'Sad, whatever,' said Kelly. 'And then she moves onto LB. Jumping around – "Oh, yay, congratulations, we're both nerds now."'

'What?' said Lockie.

'I'm telling you,' hissed Kelly. 'Réiltín heard about this, probably from Tadhg or whoever, and she didn't want to be left out—'

'No. Why would she want to be part of this?' said Lockie, raising his voice. 'Hanging out over here with a group of friends, including one who hates her, when – if it doesn't get her fired – us being up here will get her in major trouble—'

'Probably the only trouble she's ever got into in her life,' said Kelly, throwing Réiltín a dismissive glance.

Lockie held up his hands in surrender. 'In. Sane.'

Kelly walked away. 'Ass. Hole.'

Lockie turned around to Réiltín and beckoned her to come with him. He hadn't seen Kelly do a U-turn . . .

46

Réiltín froze when she saw Kelly walking towards her.

'Worst prison guard ever,' said Kelly, smiling.

'Do you have any idea how stupid this is?' said Réiltín. 'Apart from the tide about to come in, look –' she pointed up to the moon – 'there's cloud overhead, which means mist, which will make those steps you so stupidly climbed up insanely slippery to climb down. Do you have any idea?'

'I have an idea how sad you were that you weren't invited,' said Kelly.

Réiltín gave a dismissive glance. 'I don't even know what all this is.'

Kelly leaned in to her face. 'This is five tight friends wondering why a freak thinks she can join their gang.' She looked back at LB and the others, huddled in a group. 'It's probably what they're talking about right now.' She turned back to Réiltín, and put her mouth to her ear and whispered, 'And I know just what kind of a freak you are.'

Réiltín jerked her head back. 'What the hell?'

Kelly nodded slowly. 'And I don't care any more...' She glanced at the others again. 'I don't care if they all know too.'

'I don't even know what you're talking about,' said Réiltín.

'Obviously,' said Kelly. 'Otherwise you never would have come near us.'

Fear started to creep into Réiltín's eyes. Kelly gave her a broad smile, turned in the direction of the others as she reached under the back of her hoodie, into her shorts' pocket. Smiling as she started to pull something out, she turned back around to see Réiltín sitting on the grass.

'*Owww!*' screamed Réiltín, starting to stand up, her hand on the back of her head. 'Why did you *do* that?'

Kelly's mouth dropped open.

The others all charged over to them.

'Ré!' said Lockie.

Réiltín straightened up, drawing her hand slowly away from the back of her head, looking at her palm. 'Oh my God,' she said, levelling a bewildered stare at Kelly.

'What did you do?' said Lockie, glaring at Kelly, as the others gathered around.

'Me?' said Kelly. 'What? She just . . .'

Lockie pushed past her. He put his arm around Réiltín, and guided her up to the top, grabbing one of the candles for light as he gently examined the back of her head. 'No blood at least,' he said, giving her a small smile. He spun around to Kelly, who was standing, looking furious, on the fringe of the group.

'Me?' said Kelly. 'Nothing! She did that herself.'

Réiltín was looking up at Lockie, as he slowly shook his head, then turned to Kelly. 'There is something seriously wrong with you,' he said.

'Oh my God!' said Kelly. 'She's the one who—'

'What? Jumped down on the grass for the craic?' said Lockie. 'Obviously, you pushed her.'

'No, I didn't!' said Kelly. 'Why would I push her?'

'You threw her across a floor the other night,' said Lockie.

'That was an accident!' said Kelly. 'Literally, we were standing there, talking. I looked back at you guys for, like, one moment, and next thing she had flung herself on the grass.'

'Oh my God!' said LB, lunging in front of Kelly, shouting into her face. 'STOP LYING! *All the time!*'

Kelly recoiled. 'I'm not lying.'

LB stared at her. 'Did you push her?'

'No!' said Kelly. 'She—'

LB held out a hand to stop her. 'Sorry, but I'm done. I'm done with this. Just tell the truth! How hard can it be?'

Kelly stared back at LB, eyes flickering with fear.

'You liar!' said LB, stepping towards her. 'I knew it! You liar! I can see it in your eyes!'

'I'm not lying!' said Kelly. 'I swear to God! I didn't push her!'

LB glanced at Réiltín, then back at Kelly. 'What did Réiltín ever do to you?'

Everyone waited. Kelly stood there, white-faced, looking at Réiltín.

'Nothing!' said Réiltín. She pointed at Kelly. 'Admit it. I. Have. Never. Done. Anything. To. You.'

Kelly's eyes shot wide, she sucked in a huge reflexive breath, then exploded. 'You . . .' She lunged for Réiltín, but LB leaped in to protect her. Kelly, panicked, elbowed LB in the face. LB cried out, and slapped her back.

'That was an accident!' said Kelly. 'I didn't—'

LB growled and pushed Kelly hard, backwards.

'Stop!' said Kelly. 'Stop! LB! It's me. I—' She looked at Réiltín. 'She's the psycho!'

'Stop saying that!' said LB.

Lockie strode over to them. 'Everyone, calm down!'

Kelly and Réiltín had locked eyes. LB stood, dazed, between them.

Kelly burst into tears. 'I'm telling the truth.'

Lockie glanced back at her, cold and dismissive. 'Yeah, we've heard that before, Kelly.'

'*I'm* telling the truth,' said Réiltín, looking around slowly at each of the others.

Lockie held up his hands in surrender. 'Look, I just want to—'

But Kelly had ducked around Lockie and dived for Réiltín, grabbing a handful of her hoodie, pulling her down on the ground. Réiltín rolled on top of her, pinned her down, then Kelly was on top of Réiltín, Réiltín grabbing at her back to pull her off. Lockie lunged for Kelly, pulled her off Réiltín, lifted her away as she bucked against him, legs kicking.

'Let me down!' screamed Kelly, slapping his back. 'Psycho! Let me down!'

'Oh, everyone's a psycho now,' said Lockie. 'Everyone except Kelly.'

47

When everyone settled, Lockie looked around and raised his hands in surrender.

'I'm done,' he said. 'Done, done, done.' He looked at Réiltín. 'You can come with me. Can you take this from here, Rupe?'

'Absolutely not,' said Rupert.

Lockie paused, letting out a long breath. 'Well, I need to cool off.' He glared at Kelly. 'Maybe it's you I should be taking down with me.' Then he walked away.

Kelly darted after him. 'Lockie, I swear—'

He spun around to her. 'Do not follow me down here. I'm just so . . . sick of you.'

'You have no idea what a psycho she is,' said Kelly.

'Nope,' said Lockie. 'And that's all right with me.'

Réiltín started to follow Lockie down, but Kelly marched towards her. When Réiltín saw her, she backed up to the others.

'You have to be kidding me,' said LB jumping forward, taking a step towards Kelly, pulling Réiltín by her sleeve close to her side. 'Wait here.'

Kelly stared at LB. 'Oh my God – what do you think I was going to do?'

Tears sprung into her eyes. She swiped them away, then started to reach behind her again, under her hoodie.

Lockie made his way down the stone steps that curved away from the top of Carraig na nGealt. The steps were damp and slick, and he gripped on to whatever he could find to steady himself. He slipped, and grabbed onto a rock to stop his fall. Looking up, he could make out the silhouettes of the others, and held his breath when he saw how close they were to the edge. Then he saw that Rupert, with wide sweeps of his arm, was guiding them back to safety. The silhouettes disappeared, and Lockie breathed again.

Kelly turned away from the others, as she pushed her hand into the back pocket of her shorts. She frowned, searched the other one. Slowly, she looked up at Réiltín. Réiltín flashed innocent eyes at her.

'Where is it?' said Kelly.

'Where's what?' said Réiltín.

'The page!' said Kelly.

'What page?' said Réiltín.

'Oh my God – you took it out of my pocket,' said Kelly, 'when we were—' She pointed down to the ground.

Réiltín's eyes registered a yes even as she was shaking her head at the others. Kelly started to bounce on her feet.

LB stood up. 'Back away from her,' she ordered, and pointed to the right. But Kelly stepped back. 'We're going now, anyway,' said LB. She looked around to the well, where Amber was sitting on the wall, holding Rupert's hands, her bag half-packed at her feet, the selenite sphere glowing at his foot.

'There's something you need to know,' said Kelly.

'Just stop, OK?' said LB, turning back to her. 'Just stop.'

Kelly looked at Réiltín. 'Something about Réiltín,' said Kelly.

Behind LB's back, Réiltín shook her head slowly at Kelly. 'Think about it,' she said.

LB turned to her. 'Think about what? What is it?'

Réiltín locked eyes with Kelly.

'What?' said LB, looking back and forth between them, not understanding.

'Just . . .' said Réiltín, 'I think Kelly should think about whether she wants to tell another lie tonight.'

Kelly's eyes were lit with anger, her fists clenched.

'Kelly,' said LB, 'actually, you're too close to the edge. Come back further in, where it's safer.'

'I'm fine,' said Kelly, and she took two more steps back. 'What would you care, anyway?'

Rupert was drying his tears on the sleeve of Tadhg's hoodie.

'I'm sorry I didn't say anything to you about my dad earlier,' he said. 'I didn't want to ruin everything. But, as soon as Kelly did, I felt the floor was open.'

Amber smiled. 'But don't worry about your dad,' she said. 'I mean, try not to, obviously. Because he was in the hospital, they've probably done every check they could. They're letting him home . . . so that's good.'

'No, I know,' said Rupert nodding, more tears spilling.

'Oh, Rupe, is there something else?' said Amber.

Rupert shrugged. 'It's going to sound really selfish.'

'You're never selfish,' said Amber.

'Thanks,' said Rupert. 'And it wasn't like it was the first thing that came into my head when I heard about Dad . . .' He paused. 'It was more a thought that occurred to Kelly. I bumped into her just after the call, and I was upset, and she was really sweet. And then she was looking at Tadhg walking away, and she says, "Ooh. You might not be able to tell your dad now, about being . . . you know . . . because of his heart."'

280

Amber stared at Rupert, open-mouthed. 'His big, beautiful heart? Because of that? Because he might need to find some more room in it someday for someone his son loves, but it'll be a tight squeeze because it's so filled with Rupe love? That heart?' She jumped up, and stormed over to Kelly.

Rupert strode after her. 'Amber! Don't!' he called.

'What the hell did you say to Rupert earlier?' said Amber.

'About what?' said Kelly.

'About not being able to come out to his dad?' said Amber.

'I didn't say that,' said Kelly, backing away from her.

'You might as well have,' said Amber. 'He's crying over there because—'

'I didn't mean anything bad,' said Kelly.

'No, of course not,' said Amber.

Rupert moved in beside Amber, his eyes wide with fear. He took hold of her elbow. 'We're all going to step in this direction,' he said, and he gestured towards himself. 'Kelly – this way. Come my way. It's all fine. Don't look back.'

Kelly took some steps forward.

'Oh, thank God,' said Rupert. 'I can't handle this—'

'I'm serious,' said Kelly to Amber. 'I didn't mean anything bad. I was just . . . just looking out for them.

I know Rupe would never forgive himself if anything happened—'

'Because you're assuming,' said Amber, 'that his dad is going to have some terrible reaction?'

Kelly's mouth fell open. 'Coming from the girl who literally thinks there's danger around every corner! Even though *she's* the actual danger.'

Amber lunged.

48

Lockie started to walk back up the slope, slipped again, and broke his fall with his hand. He paused, his head hanging, and was about to move again when he heard raised voices above. He looked up. In the echoing screams, he saw one silhouette falling.

Réiltín and LB, white-faced, stood looking over the edge at where Kelly lay face down on a narrow spur below them.

'She landed on a ledge,' said Réiltín, turning to Amber and Rupert.

Amber was on her knees, her hands over her face, sobbing into them, as Rupert tried to comfort her.

'Is she OK?' said Amber, half turning towards the others. She started to get up, but Rupert rested his hand on her shoulder. 'We don't know yet. Stay here.'

'She moved!' said LB. 'She moved. She raised her head.'

'Kelly!' they all shouted.

'Kelly, we're coming down,' said Rupert. 'Don't worry. We're coming down to get you – everything will be OK.' He turned to the others, white-faced, pupils huge. 'LB, Réiltín – you stay up here with Amber. I'll go down.'

Amber looked up at him, her eyes pleading. 'Save her, Rupe. Please save her.'

Lockie scrambled across the coarse grass and scree towards the narrow ledge where Kelly lay. Below it, the sheer rock face, shiny and black, dropped all the way down to the sea. He reached for a handhold in front of him.

'Lockie!' Rupert shouted from above him. 'Lockie! I'm coming.'

'Don't!' said Lockie, without turning back. 'Not this way. I've got this. Follow the trail closest to you. You'll see it.' He started to slide, then righted himself, moving onto rougher ground to make a quicker, safer path to where Kelly lay.

Back at the top, Réiltín and LB sat, wide-eyed and mute, beside a sobbing Amber. After a few minutes, she sniffed and shook her head.

'We need to go down to her too,' she said. 'We *have* to.

We can't just leave her. This is all my fault. And . . . what if . . . what if anything happens to . . . to any of them down there?'

Réiltín and LB helped her to stand and propped her up between them, and half stumbling, half sliding, the three of them began following Rupert down. Ahead of them, Rupert was already making his way with Lockie towards the ledge where Kelly lay.

'Be careful, Lockie!' shouted Réiltín. 'Oh my God – she's so near the edge! She's—' She bit her lip and concentrated on putting one foot in front of the other.

Suddenly, a moan so horrifying came from the ledge below that for a moment the three girls stopped in their tracks. *Kelly!*

'We're coming, Kelly,' said Lockie. 'Don't move. We'll pull you back in.'

'No! You can't move her,' said LB. 'In case . . . her injuries.' But Réiltín pointed to the rock face below the ledge, and LB turned to her, eyes wide.

Rupert crouched down to speak to Lockie. 'And . . . how are we going to pull her in onto safer ground?' They scanned the area in front of them, desperate to know what to do.

Kelly raised her head a fraction. 'Help . . . I can't. I'm . . . I . . .'

'Hurry up!' cried Amber, struggling against her tears.

'Shut up!' shouted Lockie. 'Shut up. We've all got to think!'

'There's only one way you're going to be able to do this,' said Réiltín. 'If you lie down on your front, Lockie – you first; then you crawl across to her . . . then Rupert—'

Rocks and stones started to slide down from under Lockie's foot. His eyes widened in panic, and he dug his feet in harder. But it made it worse, and his foot took a sharp slide down. Rupert scrambled down, and grabbed on to Lockie's arm. Their breathing stopped, simultaneously, momentarily, then struck up again, fast and shallow.

'I can't watch this,' said Amber, turning away. 'This is unbearable . . .'

Kelly moaned from the ledge. 'Help . . . please . . . I'm going to fall—'

Lockie climbed higher.

'I can't,' moaned Kelly. 'I'm . . . I—'

'You can!' said LB. 'Don't speak, Kelly. Just . . . stay. Steady. They've got you. We're not going to let you fall.'

Slowly, slowly, Lockie spidered his hand towards Kelly, even that small movement sending a shower of stones down the slope. He moved closer and made a grab for Kelly's arm. As he caught it, he felt himself sliding, instinctively shot out his other hand, and yanked Rupert down with him. Rupert cried out as his hoodie snagged on a rock behind him.

'My neck!' he shouted. 'My neck.'

'Oh shit,' said LB. 'We need to get that hoodie off Rupert or he's going to choke.' She got down onto the ground and lay flat on her front, stretching out her hand as far as she could. Réiltín and Amber did the same. But they couldn't reach him from there.

'Oh, Rupert!' cried Amber. 'Oh no – no!'

Rupert managed to steady himself, pressing his back against the rock he was caught on, raising his chin to keep the pressure off his neck.

'If he slips one more time . . .' said LB.

'I think I might be able to reach him,' said Réiltín.

'And then what?' said LB.

Amber turned to her. 'Scissors. There's scissors in my backpack!'

'I'll go,' said LB.

'At the bottom,' said Amber. 'There's a hidden zip.'

LB paused. 'But are they . . . will they be strong enough to cut through?'

Amber nodded. 'Yes! Hurry!'

LB had already scrambled to her feet and was already running for it.

Kelly was looking at Lockie, her eyes filled with tears. 'Please,' she said.

'It's OK,' said Lockie. 'I'll pull you this way . . . get you safely off that. And we can get help.'

Rupert braced his back against the rock, his arm straining against Lockie's grip.

Lockie called back to him. 'Nearly there. I'll get one handhold . . .'

Réiltín appeared above Rupert, made her way down to the sharp rock that his hoodie was caught on. 'Listen. I'm going to cut this,' she said, 'because I won't be able to pull it up without choking you.' She pulled Amber's scissors from her pocket and started to cut through his hood.

'Letting go,' said Lockie. He released his grip on Rupert, and grabbed for a rock, pulling himself up a fraction. As he raised his foot to a new foothold, a slew of small stones slithered down. He swung away from Kelly. She let out another moan. Lockie spidered his fingers towards her . . .

'Lockie! You're going to go!' cried Réiltín. 'You're going to fall. Don't!'

Kelly cried out in panic.

'I won't,' said Lockie. 'I've got you, Kel. It's OK.'

Just then, Réiltín cut through the last bit of Rupert's hood, releasing the pressure around his neck. He rolled his head left and right. 'Oh, thank God! Thank you, Ré, thank you.'

But Réiltín was already watching Lockie. He started

to move his fingers towards Kelly again. Réiltín's heart pounded. Lockie made a grab for Kelly's hand, caught it, then scrambled for another foothold, higher up, found one, and released her hand again. Réiltín could see by the muscles on Lockie's neck that he was readying himself to try again.

'Lockie, it was Kelly!' blurted Réiltín. 'On the phone, earlier. Clare's father . . . he thought I was *Kelly* – not you. It was Kelly who sent Clare the texts, sent her those pictures of you . . .'

The words came spilling out.

Lockie went very still. His hand, rigid, fingers spread, stopped in the space between himself and Kelly. He turned his head slowly. He looked at Kelly. They locked eyes, Kelly's flooded with guilt and fear.

'I've got you,' he said. 'I've still got you.' His fingers kept moving. He slid again.

Réiltín turned back to Rupert, gesturing for him to follow her. She started moving down towards Lockie, and, as she did so, the front pouch of her hoodie bulged and a piece of white paper fell out, and was whipped up in the wind. It fluttered to and fro for a moment, then came to rest, caught in a tangle of branches.

Lockie, his face still turned to Kelly, was struggling to get his foot secured.

'Lockie!' said Réiltín. 'You're going to fall!'

Kelly's eyes were wide with panic.

'She won't care,' said Réiltín. 'She won't want to fall alone.'

Rupert edged closer to Réiltín.

'Lockie!' shouted Réiltín, slapping her hands on the ground.

Kelly slid, made a desperate grab for Lockie's arm, and clamped on to it. Lockie was sweating, struggling for breath.

Rupert came within reach of him, and secured himself on a shelf of rock below, wedging himself against Lockie's legs.

'Kel,' said Lockie, 'we're nearly there, OK?'

Réiltín watched, open-mouthed, shaking her head.

Lockie turned his face towards Réiltín.

'Rupe, brace yourself,' said Lockie. 'Kel, I'm giving one big pull—' Kelly started to slip, and Lockie started to slip and slide down with her. Réiltín scrambled down to his side.

'She won't want to fall alone,' said Réiltín again, this time quieter.

Above them, a gust of wind blew the sheet of paper free from where it was snagged, and it floated down into the space between Kelly and Réiltín. Kelly didn't see Réiltín raise the scissors and bring the blades down hard into the back of her hand, then rip them out again.

Kelly released her grip, and disappeared, horrifyingly silently, down the dark rock into the sea, a single sheet of white paper floating after her, scissors soon to follow.

EPILOGUE

Rupert stood on the docks at Port Hercules, his gleaming hair tidy-tousled, bobbing yachts reflected in the amber lenses of his tortoiseshell Wayfarers. He was dressed in an ivory three-piece suit, white shirt and white textured leather sneakers. He turned when he heard the clank of bracelets and saw Amber in a baggy top and long, white baggy trousers, walking towards him. Her hair was short and bleached blonde, her sunglasses blush-coloured with smoky lenses.

They stood, for a moment, in silence.

'I *am* someone, you know,' said Rupert, gesturing to his outfit.

'Oh,' said Amber. 'I thought that was dress-code obedience.'

'Hey,' said Lockie, walking towards them, tugging at his white short-sleeved shirt. He stood beside Amber, head lowered, struggling to re-button it.

Amber reached up. 'That might help.' She slid off his sunglasses, and examined them. 'Nice.'

'Rupert picked them for me,' said Lockie.

Amber smiled. She passed the glasses back to Lockie. He put them on and exchanged a gentlemanly nod with Rupert.

They all scanned each other's outfits.

'Amber,' said Rupert, 'looks like she's about to fumigate your home. Lockie looks like he's crew.'

'And Rupert,' said Amber. 'Looks—'

'Is,' said Rupert, '*L'Arnacoeur*, eponymous heartbreaker from the 2010 film starring Romain Duris and Vanessa Paradis, set against . . . ?'

He swept an arm backwards to where the Rock of Monaco towered over them.

Amber ducked in beside him, so that when he brought his arm back, it was around her shoulder. She pulled Lockie in at the other side.

They stood, in silence, hidden eyes ahead.

The yacht moved slowly through the water. Ash Warner, dressed in a billowing white maxi dress, face damp with tears, sat holding the white paper urn filled with her daughter Kelly's ashes and handwritten farewell messages from family and friends.

'This is an extremely difficult day,' said Ash. 'For all of us. And I want to thank everyone for being here. And, obviously, thank Antsy and Trish for hosting us.'

Trish squeezed Antsy's hand.

Ash smiled around at everyone. 'Life is so . . . It's so hard and quiet without Kelly. The house . . .' She started to cry and then she started to laugh. 'Well, it's so tidy!' She paused. 'And so empty. And it doesn't get the sun anymore.'

She looked across at Rupert, and Lockie, and Amber, and LB.

'You know,' said Ash. 'You were her best friends. She was crazy and wild, and she loved you all.'

Ash let out a breath. 'OK. Let's do this. Let's set my wild flower free.' She burst into tears.

LB burst into tears. Lockie jerked around, grabbed on to the railing, leaned over the side of the yacht and threw up. Rupert passed him his handkerchief. Lockie wiped his streaming eyes with it, clung to the railing, head bowed over the side.

Amber scanned the emotional chaos.

Danger! Rockfalls!

Stop!

Lies Are Like Loose Rocks.

The yacht hit a wave, and they all lifted in their seats, and they all grabbed for the railing.

'So . . . "rise above the lies" – that's the message,' Rupert had said. 'Or hold tight to them, so they don't get loose in the first place.'

They all held tight.

Réiltín appeared on the terrace of the Behans' villa, carrying a tray with five glasses of fresh lemonade, each with a striped paper straw. Below her, in the garden, was the row of loungers she had carefully arranged, spaced six feet apart, facing the house. She looked down at her reclining friends – Rupert, Lockie, LB and Amber – all silent, all dressed in white, all wearing sunglasses.

Réiltín carried the tray down the stone steps, ice cubes clinking, footsteps silent. She crossed the garden, behind the loungers, and set the tray on a table in the shade. She picked up a drink and went to the first lounger. She crouched down, lay a gentle hand on Lockie's forearm and leaned in close. 'I hope you don't feel guilty,' she said, handing him his drink. 'I was the one who did it. Yes, you told me to. But I'm the only one who saw you mouth –' she leaned in closer and breathed – 'Do it.' She pulled slowly back. 'To everyone else,' she whispered, 'it looked exactly as it was: I was saving your life.'

She squeezed his arm, collected the next drink and moved to the next lounger. She crouched down, lay a gentle hand on Amber's forearm and leaned in close. 'I hope you don't feel guilty,' she said, handing her the drink. 'I was the one who did it. Yes, none of it would have happened if you hadn't lunged for Kelly. But I couldn't have saved Lockie's and Rupert's lives without your sneaky scissors.' She squeezed Amber's arm, collected the next drink and moved to the next lounger.

She crouched down.

'A moment,' said Rupert. He pressed his back against the lounger and, with a thumb and forefinger, raised his Wayfarers to his forehead, to see what was emerging beyond her: Tadhg, from the pool. *Like a statue that had fallen into it but was kissed by a handsome merman and brought to life. Then dressed in short-short swim trunks in a deep shade of petrol blue, with a snug waistband featuring decorative button and faux fly. And lo, the first thing this chiselled— No, this . . . anthropomorphic carving noticed when he stepped onto dry land was oil suitable for use on wet skin and as he reached for it . . .*

LB crossed Rupert's line of vision as she swept past him. He sighed and sat up, nodded at Réiltín.

She lay a gentle hand on his forearm, and leaned in close. 'I hope you don't feel guilty,' she said, handing him his drink. 'I was the one who did it. Yes, if you hadn't told Amber about your conversation with Kelly, she wouldn't have lunged for her, but you loved Tadhg. Even back then. The idea of having to keep that a secret, the idea of not having Tadhg in your life for *any* reason . . . that's upsetting. He's my best friend – I get it.' She glanced over at Tadhg. 'Because we all know how Tadhg feels about secrets.' She smiled. '"The End".'

Réiltín squeezed Rupert's arm and walked away, then made a swift change in direction. Rupert watched her arrive at the pool, suddenly, it seemed, holding a large, neatly folded bright orange towel that she shook out for Tadhg. She smiled over her shoulder at Rupert as Tadhg rolled himself into it, then into her arms, laughing.

He couldn't be sure she hadn't noticed the solid footing he was on that night, the firm grip he had on a protruding rock above him, how he could then hook his arm under Kelly's legs, securing them. Nor could he be sure she hadn't heard him say, 'I'm solid, I have her, she can't take you down' and that all it would have taken to lower Kelly to safety was a gentle release of her grip.

Tadhg looked up and gave Rupert a huge happy wave. Rupert mirrored it.

Never The End. Please, Never The End.

LB walked down the terrace steps and across the garden. Réiltín left Tadhg when LB was settled on her lounger, and brought her her drink.

She crouched down, lay a gentle hand on LB's forearm, and leaned in close. 'I hope you don't feel guilty,' she said, handing her the drink. 'I was the one who did it. Yes, you pushed Kelly off the cliff, but how were you supposed to know there was a ledge underneath? She should have just plunged to her death. Yes, if you hadn't done that, I wouldn't have had to stab Kelly's hand with Amber's scissors to save Lockie's life, but equally . . . yours. Kelly and I were the only ones who saw the pause. I'm the only one who knew it was deliberate. There were five of us up there, pushing and pulling, and you chose push. Can you imagine if I didn't do what I did, though? I can't imagine Kelly would have agreed to sit around with us for five hours to "learn the truth" that it was an accident.' Réiltín stood up, walked around the back of LB's lounger, and put her hands on LB's shoulders.

She looked across at the terrace. She noticed a curved bay window on the villa that she hadn't seen the last time she was there, all those years ago. The old terrace had been redesigned, but that window looked like it might have had a view over something she really didn't think anyone could have seen, especially because almost everyone was at the birthday party. Everyone except her. She had been crouched in a corner by the bushes, writing, then skipping away, then coming back to watch what happened next.

Réiltín squeezed LB's shoulders and walked away, across the garden, up the terrace steps and around the corner under the window. Voices came from above.

'Listen, Antsy,' said Ash. 'I do appreciate you hosting this. That's not the point.'

Réiltín froze and backed up against the wall. She looked up. The window was open a crack.

'All I was commenting on,' said Ash, 'was that this – today, with the rest of the gang here – was strange. Uncomfortable. OK? The last time those kids were here was when Jeremy "fell" and cracked his head open, but was "Fine, guys! Don't worry! Let's all go to the funfair!"'

'Look,' said Antsy, 'that boy had a funeral fit for a king. And LB wasn't scarred for life by a little boy dying at her birthday party in a game *she* made everyone play. I made sure *none* of our kids were scarred.'

'Even Caruvi's girl? Was she not stashed down the garden with all her mannequins, when her mother was making tour costumes?'

Réiltín nodded, her heart beating faster. *She was. Stashed away. But it didn't mean she stayed there.*

'Keep your voice down!' hissed Antsy. 'And come down a fraction off the moral high ground, because

I couldn't have done any of it without you. You had no problem wiping down the railing someone had oiled up. No problem getting rid of the blood-stained clue that told him to climb over it.'

'Shut up,' hissed Ash. 'You know why I did that. That was about securing a future! For me and my daughter! I knew Mark was about to leave us. I didn't ask you for a single penny, just to keep my job. And I'm damn good at it and you know it.' She paused. 'And stop trying to convince me none of the kids were scarred. Kelly was hysterical. I think she saw what happened.'

'Did you ever talk about it again?' said Antsy.

'Are you mad?' said Ash. 'I scared the living daylights out of her to make sure she'd keep quiet. I told her if she ever spoke about it, she'd never be able to come back here, that she couldn't be friends with LB, that you could go to jail and I'd lose my job. We swore to never, ever mention that day again.'

'But you didn't tell her he died,' said Antsy.

'No,' said Ash. 'None of them know!'

Réiltín's eyes widened. *Except Kelly. The night she died. Having the Lodge to herself, reminded of Jeremy's existence, looking him up, printing out his obituary, folding it up into her little back pocket to confront the girl who did it, tell her she was a killer now, not just someone who cracked a boy's*

300

head open, tell all her friends that she was Twinkle, Twinkle Big Freak now.

'Well, whoever did it,' said Antsy, 'I'm sure they didn't think he was going to die.'

Or maybe they just . . . didn't care.

ACKNOWLEDGEMENTS

To the wildly talented Rachel Denwood, Managing Director at Simon & Schuster Children's Books, thank you for this glorious adventure.

Thank you to the excellent Lowri Ribbons, Fiction Editor at Simon & Schuster Children's Books.

Thank you to my outstanding agent, Eve White at Eve White Literary Agency.

Thank you to the brilliant Ludo Cinelli at Eve White Literary Agency.

Thank you, Lizzie Clifford, Sarah Hall and Leena Lane for working your magic.

To Rónán Mac Con Iomaire, thank you for your invaluable and inspiring contribution.

To Flora Lyons, you absolute joy of a human being.

Thank you for your wisdom and wit.

To Sam Lynch, thank you for services to research and author entertainment.

To Paula Kavanagh, thank you for your multi-level support, eagle eye and intuition.

To PJ Lynch, thank you for your kindness, encouragement, generosity and laughter.

To Julie Sheridan, thank you, once again, for being so giving with your big heart and your big brain, every step of the way.

To Jenny Murphy, thank you for your extraordinary healing ways.

Thank you to my gorgeous friends on the RPK road – Sue Booth-Forbes of Anam Cara Writers' and Artists' Retreat, David and Majella Geraghty and awesome family, Mary Harrington Causkey, Ger Holland, Liz Nugent and Richard McCullough, Sue Swansborough and Brian Williams.

Thank you to my beloved family.